I0535609

FRESH OUT

CAUJUAN AKIM MAYO

ISBN: 0692541713
ISBN-13: 978-0692541715
www.uprockpublications.com

DEDICATION

This book is dedicated to my loving mother
Queen. May you forever rest in peace

ACKNOWLEDGEMENTS

Shout out to all my supporters and people that believed in me: My son Raa'Quan and Duffy. D-Roll. Brothers Allmighty, Hakiem, Rayshon, Self and Reality. To my relative Kemo, sister Yanai. All of my nieces and nephews. My aunt Laqueesha and Jeanne. My beautiful caring and loving mother Queen, may you forever rest in peace.
To my true friends Atoy, Juveseve, Jon, and Jay Jay. Ya'll my day one niggas. To all the Skyline homies, P patna's, and females that held me down. Lena, Stefanie, Jennifer, Shea and Leisha.
To my friends I've known for 10 years plus, Kadeve, Maroy, Bill, Marcell, Miesha, Big June, and anyone I may have forgotten to mention, insert name here _____. Last but not least, I would like to send a super shout out to any and everybody locked up, doing time. Keep your head up, stay strong, and I pray you make it home safe.

1 SHORT TIME

"Won't be long now gangsta. What you got, like 3 weeks?"

"Yeah, bout dat." J-Bone answered his celly while sitting on his bunk reading an XXL. Jamal Hicks. That was J-Bone's government name. Jamal was just finishing up a six year bid for armed robbery. He'd just gotten his S. Time (short time) ducat at mail call which meant it was official. He was set to be released 2 weeks from today, January 22, 2013. It had been a long six years but Jamal handled it like a solider. Almost everyone that Jamal put his trust into, with the exception of his mom, let him down, turned their backs on him, or never kept in touch. He tried not to take it personal and would always remind himself that this was the nature of the beast. And when you're in the belly of it, people tend to forget about you. Out of site, out of mind. Your life stopped but the rest of the worlds' kept moving. It's a hard pill to swallow but it's the truth and Jamal learned this early into his sentence when his girlfriend of two years, "Jessica" left him for the dead, stopped writing and visiting six months after his sentencing and started fucking with his best friend, Dee.

"What's the first thing you gonna do when you get out?" His celly Brain Dead asked while making a Top Ramen soup with cheese and crackers in it, also known as a spread. Brain Dead had been down for 18 years. He got his nickname from smoking too much sherm in the 90's. One day, during one of his usual smoke sessions, he had a bad trip and started hallucinating.

He thought his long time girlfriend was the devil and out to get him, so he smashed her face in with a hammer while she was sleep.

Then the story got weird. The police pulled up on Brain Dead a block away from his house down the street, running, talking in tongues, with blood and brain matter on his clothes. Apparently, Brain Dead had started eating his girl's brains after he killed her. Jamal never asked him about it.

"Shit, get me some pussy!" They both laughed.

"Other than that nigga."

"Nah, I know what you're saying," Jamal said then continued. "I'm a go out there and try and find a job. The street life ain't gonna do shit but land me back in here, so I'm done with that."

"Real talk, I feel you on that playboy."

"And I'm staying the fuck out the set and away from the homies!" Jamal was from Skyline Piru. A notorious blood set out of San Diego. That's where he got his name "J-Bone" from. A lot of blood's nicknames ended in Bo, Ru, or Bone. Jamal was a real factor from Skyline. He was known to put it down at all cost, fearless and bout the business.

"Now that's the realist shit I heard you say

all day," Brain Dead responded.

"Blood, I'm so bool on the homies it ain't even funny. Too many niggas out there snitchin and hatin on each other while these cross town niggas is gettin money. Blood, if I haven't known you for at least 10 years or better, then I ain't tryna know you. These new young niggas from a different era. They lack the true guidance, respect, and knowhow that was instilled in us growing up by our OG's"

"I feel you on that J-Bone, but at the same time, like you said, they don't know any better, so it's up to us to teach em."

"Yeah I guess. All I know is I'm keeping my circle tight. I've always been that way. Survival 101."

"As you should," Brain Dead said and agreed as they were interrupted by the sound of a C.O. over the loud speaker and the cracking of cell doors announcing that it was yard time.

xxx

"CDC number?" The C.O. asked Jamal as he

undressed out of his prison garbs and put on his dress outs.

"T–23693," Jamal responded. The C.O. wrote down Jamal's number and prisoner info on a small pad, then went to the other end of the hall to process him out. The process took a little under an hour. Three other inmates were paroling as well. A mexican and two brothers. Everyone was happy and excited to be getting out finally and going home. One of the brothers that was being released had been down for over 10 years.

While down, every one of his loved ones that he cared about had passed away, including his mother, the only person that had been down for him throughout his incarceration, and 8 months before his release date, she lost her battle with cancer and passed away. That's one of the hardest things to deal with when you're locked up. Losing loved ones and not being able to attend their funerals, find closure or say goodbye. This was something that Jamal always feared, losing his mother while being locked up.

"Okay. Everyone line up." The C.O. said, as

he opened the cell door holding each of the parolees' prison ID and release papers. They all got up simultaneously like an assembly full of school kids rising for the Pledge of Allegiance. Jamal couldn't wait ta get up out of there. He could smell freedom on the tip of his nose like fresh breakfast in the morning. The C.O. loaded Jamal and the 3 other parolees into a van and drove them a few yards to the front gate where inmates are received and released. *I can't wait ta get up out this mutha fucka,* Jamal thought to his self, as the van slowly approached the prison release gate and came to a stop.

XXX

"Wuss up, Cuzz?"

"Nigga, I ain't cha cousin." Jamal responded to the nigga that stood before him.

"What chu sayin then Cuzz?"

"Blood, I'm from Skyline Piru. Keep smuzzin me Blood and we can take it to the pocket."

"Fuck the pocket!!!" The Crip took off with a sloppy right. Now they were in a fist fight.

Jamal saw the right hook coming a mile away. He anticipated it from the moment the nigga disrespected him. He done took off on way too many niggas himself not ta know the get down. Jamal stepped back like Muhammad Ali doing the Rope-A-Dope, then leaped forward with two quick jabs. **Wap Wap!** The crip nigga never saw it coming.

"Now wut BLOOD? You can't fuck wit me Ru!" Jamal said to the man on the floor that laid before him, holding his mouth and eye simultaneously with one hand in a daze like he just took sleeping pills. Just at that moment, five other bloods walked up, one of them being Brain Dead, and introduced themselves. They blood shook hands and embraced as J-Bone had earned his respect. That was his first day in prison. From that day forth, he had no more problems, unless he started it himself. With every bone crushing, teeth shattering, nose broken fight he inflicted upon his victims, he earned his respect within the prison system and a reputation that would help him survive his sentence with minimal drama, politics and conflict. J-Bone ran with the San Diego Blood Car on the yard, a mix of various different blood sets from Daygo (San Diego), all united while in prison riding for a common cause...That blood life!

XXX

"Alright fellas, everyone out. You're no longer prisoners and property of CDC. Go off and become productive citizens. Fuck up and fall back into the life...And I'll be here ta greet your ass when you return."

The sound of the C.O. talking snapped Jamal out of his daze. The van emptied out quicker than a building full of elementary kids on the last day of school. Nobody was at the gate to pick up Jamal because he didn't let anyone know that he was being released. Not even his mother. He wanted to walk in and surprise her. As for his friends, he wanted to keep a low pro and distance from them. He loved his homies and would do anything for them, but he knew it would be hard to stay on the straight and narrow hangin and bangin in the set.

That was just a one way ticket back to prison. A place that Jamal vowed he'd never step foot again. The bus station wasn't that far from the prison and was where parolees that didn't have gate pick ups were let out. J-Bone was the only one who didn't have a pick up so he was the only one shuttled a few miles further to the Greyhound bus station.

2 WELCOME HOME

Jamal arrived at his mother's house right off of Norm St. and Skyline Dr. He crept to the front door trying to catch his mother by surprise. He tried the handle but it was locked. He noticed her car in the driveway so he knew she was home. He put his finger over the peep hole and rung the door bell. **DING DONG!**

"Coming," Said Mama Hicks, from the other side of the door as she approached, while wiping her hands on a dishrag after placing a fresh pan of homemade biscuits in the oven.

"Who is it?" Mama Hicks asked, looking through the peep hole while seeing nothing but darkness due to the fact that Jamal was covering it up.

"It's UPS. I have a large package that requires your signature ma'am." Jamal disguised his voice as he tricked his mother into opening the door. Momma Hicks thought the darkness she was seeing through the peephole was just the package in the mailman's hands in front of the door covering it up. She opened up the door, in which time, to her amazement, time seemed to have slowed down as she saw her one and only son standing before her.

"Hi Momma." Jamal walked over to hug his mom, smiling ear to ear like the Joker. She couldn't even speak. She was so shocked to see her son and filled with so much appreciation, that all she could do was hug him back as tears of joy that her boy was home flowed down her loving face.

"They finally let my baby out that cage. When did you get released?"

"Early this morning, like ten or so. I took the bus so it took a minute but I came straight here."

"Why didn't you tell me you was getting out? I could have picked you up."

"That's exactly why I didn't tell you, cause I didn't want you driving all that way trying to pick me up. Plus, I wanted to surprise you." He smiled and kissed his mother on the cheek.

"Well I'm just glad you're home baby. And just in time, too."

"Is that my momma's biscuits?" Jamal asked, sounding like Martin from the old school sit-com in the 90's.

"Boy that nose of yours always was able to smell my biscuits. Through a pot of pig feet cooking, stuffed nose, two miles away in a manure factory, you could make out your momma's biscuits."

"You damn right..."

"Boy watch your mouth."

"Sorry momma." They both laughed, hugged again, then went inside and got reacquainted as Jamal munched on his momma's biscuits.

XXX

The next day Jamal woke up bright and early to see his parole officer. This was all new to Jamal and he wasn't trying to go back to prison for showing up late to report. *Nope, I'm done with that life*, he thought to himself as he fixed his tie, looking in the mirror, reflecting on the time he spent in prison. He snapped out of it and got his mind back on the here and now. It was only his second day out so prison was still very fresh in his head. He knew then it was gonna take time to shake the prison mentality and way of thinking.

Time before he could feel comfortable with another man standing close to him without feeling threatened or some type of way. Time before he could see the good in people and not the savage brutal acts and demons some of us possess. Time before he could get used to eating his food slow and enjoying the meal without the restraints of a time limit or controlled feeding. Time before he could take the little things in life for granted again, like the smell of bacon in the morning or taking a shit in private without the company of another full grown man present. Oh yeah, it was gonna take time to get used to these things and a lot of others for that matter, but Jamal was determined to succeed. Failure was not an option. He would tell himself, 'No matter how hard life might be on the streets, it's nowhere near as hard as it is in prison. So if you can survive that, then you can survive this.'

Jamal told himself that one last time in the mirror as he finished getting ready and headed out the door to see his P.O. He didn't have a car yet so he had to leave himself enough time to catch the bus. Jamal made his way up the street and around the corner to catch the bus by Moonlight Liquor Store. Back in the 80's and 90's, Moonlight used to be one of the #1 hangout spots for the East Side Piru Skyline Bloods, the very same set Jamal belonged to.

Now because of police enforced gang injunctions, any known gang members caught hanging out by the store would be immediately arrested for violation. If you was on parole or probation, it could mean 12 new months in prison. Jamal wasn't trying to hear that so he made his way straight to the bus stop and sat down. Never once even thinking about buying so much as a cold soda to quench his thirst on the hot day. Fuck that. He'll die of thirst before he even think about setting a foot into the store.

Jamal just hoped he didn't run into one of the homies. He knew the chances of not was slimmer than Snoop Dogg on Jenny Craig and crack combined. Just as he thought about not running into one of the homies, he ended up making his thoughts a reality, thinking it into existence and doing just that.

"Blood, is that J-Bone?" A voice from across the street with a bright red shirt and matching chucks said, one hand up above his eyes like he was trying to make out a face. Jamal recognized his voice from the first word. It was Killa, his childhood friend he grew up with. Killa lived around the corner from Jamal on Royal Oak by the park. When they were young, they would pull beer runs at Moonlight and get faded in the park.

"Wuss up Killa? Yeah, it's me." Jamal responded.

"Hell yeah, they fuckin let my real one out of the box," Killa said with excitement, crossing the street with a smile on his face like his best friend just got out of prison. "When did you get home blood?"

"Today, but I'm tryna keep it on the hush. I don't want too many niggas knowing I'm out, especially Dee." Jamal was still pissed off about Dee fucking his girl Jessica and claiming her as his chick while he was down. He knew that when they ran into each other it was on and popping. Dee broke the code...bros before hoes.

"Yeah I feel you blood. Damn homie, you got big as fuck! What you benching, like 300?"

Jamal laughed and said, "I don't know, you know they took the weights out the penitentiary years ago. This is all pull-ups, push ups, and dips here baby." Jamal said, while flexing his muscles like a body builder on the Santa Monica Pier. "All bar work."

"Damn blood, I need to get my ass back in the gym. You making me look bad." Jamal gave a slight laugh at Killa's last comment and then switched subjects. "Blood, you see Jessica around?" Killa "had" seen Jessica around. It was a known fact that she was Dee's woman now.

Dee was Killa's homeboy just like Jamal and didn't wanna get in the middle of their love triangle. He knew that matters of the heart could turn deadly. Look what happened to O.J. Simpson. He wanted no parts in that conversation so he downplayed what he knew.

"Yeah I saw her a couple times. Once at the Marley Fest and another time at the set picnic." The truth of the matter was Killa had seen Jessica just about every day. Yep, every day. Sitting right on the passenger side of Dee's ride. There was no way Killa was gonna tell that to Jamal, though, so he left that little tidbit out.

"Is that right?" Jamal asked, one eyebrow raised, eyeing Killa suspiciously like he knew it was more to the story. But he didn't press on and Killa was happy he hadn't. Killa just ignored his last comment like he said nothing. Before he could switch subjects, Jamal said, "well if you see her or Dee, especially that nigga Dee, don't tell em I'm home."

"Fa sho. So what's your plans now that you're out?" Killa asked, trying to quickly get off the Dee and Jessica topic and on to something more positive and less touchy.

"First and foremost, I gotta find a job because living at mom's house ain't gonna cut it. I'm a grown ass man. Shit, I turn 31 in December."

"Nigga, it's January!"

"So what, you get the point." They both laughed. "Naw, I feel you blood." Killa responded, with a serious and all joking to the side look on his face. "Yeah, we too old now, Ru. Gotta make a better way for our children..." Jamal interrupted him.

"Nigga I ain't got no kids!" They both laughed.

"Well I do. Five kids and five baby mommas. Shit maybe the six one I'll get it right."

"Damn nigga, you ain't done having kids yet?" Jamal questioned in disbelief.

"Nope, got one on the way with Falisha."

"Falisha from the set?"

"Yep, what other Falisha you know?"

"You wrong for that one gangsta."

"Hey, keep it in the set." They both laughed and shook hands as Jamal's bus arrived and stopped in front of them. "Alright homie, be easy. I'll get with you," Killa said, as he one arm hugged his homie he hadn't seen in over five years.

"Alright homie. Remember, keep me being out on the low. Matter of fact, just keep it to yourself." Killa agreed and Jamal got on the bus.

3 TRYING TO MAKE IT

"Here, take this cup and go piss in it. Leave the door open." The Parole Officer instructed Jamal. *Damn, he really just gonna stand over my shoulder peter gazing*, Jamal thought to himself as the officer watched him unzip his pants and remove his penis and pee before leaving to make sure Jamal wasn't concealing anything false or using fake urine.

Jamal pissed in the cup, sealed the top with a plastic cap the P.O. gave him, and signed the top. Standard procedure. Next, the P.O. took a picture of Jamal and all of his tattoos, especially the gang ones. That was how they documented and identified you throughout the system and the streets.

If you jumped parole this would help find you. If you went on the run, this would help find you. Committed a crime...well, you get the picture. Jamal had a pretty cool P.O. He was fair but firm. Do what you supposed to do, stay out of trouble, find and keep a job, stay away from other gang members, ex-cons and parolees, and don't give him any dirties. Some would say that was a lot to comply with, but not if you was serious about changing your life around for the better. Jamal saw this as a perfect opportunity to do better. Stay on the straight and narrow. To be a productive citizen for the first time in his 23 years on the planet. To find an actual job that didn't require him to look over his shoulder, run from the law, or carry a gun to protect and kill someone.

Jamal finished up with his P.O. and went to look for a job. His P.O. informed him that he would be coming by his mother's house to do a home visit sometime that week and to be home when he does. Jamal agreed and got on his way. Upon going to prison, traditional methods of finding a job was still effective. You know, Sunday classifieds, help wanted, etc. But here it was 2013 and a lot had changed in a short amount of time. Now everything was done online. Jamal figured this lesson out quick when every place he tried to apply for work directed him to their website and online job submission form page.

Jamal wasn't too computer savvy, nor did he own a computer, so hence the problem he had at first looking and applying for a job. He learned and adapted quickly, though, via his new smart phone that he copped from Metro PCS after leaving his P.O's office with half the money he had gotten from being released. The other half he spent on a couple outfits, and when I say a "couple," they were just that... a couple.

3 Months Later...

Nothing much had changed in Jamal's life with the exception that he was beginning to grow impatient with being broke. He had been laying low at his mom's house while trying to find a job. Needless to say, he had been unsuccessful in landing one. He even tried Labor Finders, a construction temp agency that hired just about anybody and everybody that was willing to work and swing a hammer.

Unless that hammer swinger was a convicted ex-con seeking employment with their company. Then it was, "Hi, my name is Jamal Hicks. I came in last week and filled out an application with your company to work. I was just touching basis to see if you had a chance to look over my application, and if so, had any jobs available which fit my background and criteria?"

Every time, it was, "sorry but we lost your application, can you please come in and fill out another one?" Or, "sorry, but at the moment we have no jobs available till next month. Try back next week." *Why would I try back next week if you just said you wouldn't have anything available till next month?* Jamal said to himself.

This was the type of stuff Jamal had been going through. No one was hiring. It was a recession. And the little few companies that were hiring wasn't trying to hire an ex-felon. So needless to say, Jamal's choices were very limited. Still being, he kept his head up and remained positive. More importantly, he didn't give up or fall back into his old ways and life of crime.

"**Wuss up Blood!**" a voice yelled out from Skyline Park as Jamal walked passed the rec.

"Who's that?" Jamal asked, eyes quenched one hand over his forehead trying to make out the face.

"It's Killa Blood"

"Oh wuss poppin Ru!"

"Nothin much. Just bickin back smokin this blunt and gettin faded," Killa responded while taking the last hit of the blunt and flicking it to the ground as he greeted Jamal with a one arm hug and P shake. Jamal reluctantly shook his hand back, knowing that if he was to get pulled over by gang unit, he was sure to get violated. Getting caught hanging with a gang member was an instant 12 month violation back to the penitentiary. That was a ride Jamal was not trying to take again, especially over something so simple, "Stay - away - from -

the – homies."

But it wasn't that simple. He was a factor from Skyline Piru. He lived in the heart of the set. How could he seriously avoid contact day to day with another documented gang member while living under these conditions and circumstances?

"Blood, let's walk across the street Ru and take it to the pad. I don't mind bickin it indoors with a select few of my real ones, but outside is a no no homie. The set is hot and I can't afford a violation," Jamal said as Killa responded.

"I feel you blood. I'm actually on probation myself. I just happen ta don't give a fuck." They both laughed as they crossed the street and took it to the house.

"Blood, I need to find a job Ru," Jamal said, as he and Killa sat down on the couch and chopped it up.

"Well I got a job we can do right now that a set you right for at least six months."

"Naw blood, I ain't even tryna go that route. I'd be lying if I said the thought hadn't crossed my mind, but I can't afford to go back to the pen behind some dumb shit."

"I feel you Ru gang," Killa said, then continued, "but I wouldn't hit you wit no bullshit. This a clean lick blood for two bricks at least, maybe more. And the nigga's a mark. Straight busta, think he from the set. Blood we could just D.Bo the nigga on some G shit, or we could go all masked up on some professional shit. Either way, it's a clean lick."

"Blood, I ain't wit jackin no homies." Jamal responded.

"Naw this nigga grew up in Pacific Beach. He supplies that whole area. Got PB on lock. Them white boys treat him like God up there and got him really believing it."

"Is that right? Shit, I ain't gonna lie, it sound tempting. This living off momma shit ain't the business. I need ta make something happen, and quickly. Before hittin a nigga like this buster off becomes another day and daily ritual like waking up and morning breakfast."

"Yea dat!" See Jamal was a stick up kid by trade and nothing was off limits. If it made dollars, then it made sense. But he favored hitting drug dealers and busters because who was they gonna run to, the cops? Yeah right, and tell em what, that they just got robbed for their drugs and guns? Not likely. So Jamal always looked at it as *fuck it, let's keep it street. I robbed a street nigga on some street nigga shit. Now if he feel some type of way at the end of the day, he's more than welcome ta come see me, "equally," on some street shit, however he see fit.*

That was Jamal's way of looking at it. He feared no one. He wasn't foolish and picked his targets wisely. He didn't have a death wish but he didn't give a fuck as well. If shit went wrong and somehow the person he was jackin or jacked found out it was him who did it, Jamal was always prepared with that gun play to take it to the next level if his victims ever dared to come a knocking.

Jamal shook away the thought of taking Killa up on his offer and said, "So what's up for the weekend? I need some pussy like Al Sharpton need his hairline back." Killa laughed and said, "There's a party this weekend at Red's house. It's supposed ta be turnt up, hella active! But I know you ain't tryna fuck with that. All the homies is gonna be there.

And where there's homies…there's set rats."

"Yea I know, but that's definitely not the place ta be for me. Not to mention, I'm sure Dee's gonna be up there at the party and probably with Jessica. If so, he gonna be feeling himself and might come at me sideways. If he did, ain't no telling what I'd do."

"Blood, you gotta stop trippin off that bitch Ru and let it go." Killa said to Jamal, looking him dead in his eyes with all sincerity.

"It ain't even bout the bitch homie. It's about respect! I expect the bitch to snake me because bitches do what bitches do but Dee was my homeboy. I grew up with that nigga since first grade, Mr McFinnley's class back row."

"Damn nigga, took it back to grade school." Killa joked.

"Fuck you!" Jamal jokingly responded, smiling with a slight smirk giving Killa the bird. "You know what I mean."

"Yeah, I'm just fuckin wit you gangsta." Word had hit the streets that Jamal was out and felt some type of way about his old homie and ex bitch Jessica. Everyone was waiting and anticipating the outcome once the two came face to face for the first time since Jamal's release.

XXX

"Yeah baby suck this dick...emm." Dee said with a slight moan semi sounding like a bitch as Jessica sucked his dick like a porn star on porn hub.

"You like that Daddy?"

"Hell yeah boo, you already know," Dee responded, head back, biting his lips with his toes curled. He was about to bust a nut. Jessica sensed it and pulled his dick out her mouth as if she had cum radar, because no sooner than he pulled out of her mouth, Dee skeeted all over her tits, as she jacked him off and relinquished the remainder of his protein onto her body. Jessica could suck a mean dick but she didn't swallow. Nope, not her. It was the one flaw Dee hated about her. But he was determined to break her. Little did he know that she had already been broken, long before he came along. The only man she never had pull out her mouth was Jamal. The true love of her life. But once he got locked up, it was out of sight, out of mind.

Jessica was about her money so when Jamal's best friend Dee came sniffing around in disguise as a friendly shoulder to cry on after Jamal got locked up, she played slow like a blonde bitch with Hugh Hefner in the Playboy mansion, all the while knowing that Dee was about his money and getting it in a real way. After Jamal got locked up and sentenced, love had nothing to do with nothing when it came to men, other than Jamal. Men was a toy to be played with. A tool if you will. She used them to keep her bills paid and closet laid. Not to mention, she had a cold weed habit and she didn't smoke that reggie. Never that! In San Diego, California? Shiiit! Even the homeless smoke that loud.

Jessica was a bad bitch, Puerto Rican and Black with natural long hair to the middle of her back. Flawless smooth skin with exotic cheekbones like Kim Kardashian mixed with Halle Berry and Mariah Carey. And to set it all off, she had an ass like Nicki Minaj, minus the injections. They didn't make em like her in the hood, and that's why every nigga in the set wanted to get with that, make her wifey and lock her down. But she wasn't going for that. Whoever she got with was gonna have to pay like he lay. No free pussy this way. And Dee's sucka for love fit the bill perfectly. Jessica had his nose wide open. He'd do anything for her, outside of some gay shit.

Dee used to be Jamal's right hand man. Anytime Jamal put down a lick, you could best believe Dee was right on the side of him with that thang thang, ready to let loose if anybody didn't listen or move. Dee was a live wire, a real "brazy" ass nigga, as the homies would say from time to time, behind some of his actions. Dee was a reputable homie from the set. He was the same age as Jamal. They made names for themselves coming up through the ranks of Skyline's notorious.

"Damn girl, you suck a mean dick, but you need to start swallowing." Dee said, as he pulled up his pants, zipped up and tightened his belt.

"Hell naw nigga, I told you already, that's nasty."

"Ain't nothing nasty about it girl, that's protein."

"Then you drink it nigga!"

"Bitch watch yourself," Dee responded in a playful manner as they both laughed then lifted the seats back up in Dee's Escalade, windows fogged up sitting in Skyline Park. Dee wiped the inside windshield with his hand in a circular motion to clear the dew. Low and behold to his surprise, he saw Jamal across the street with the homie Killa.

XXX

"Let me walk you out Ru," Jamal said, as he opened the door and followed Killa to the streets. Jamal walked to the corner with the homie, gave him a P shake and told him, "B-up," all the while not noticing the black escalade across the street which held the two people that betrayed him the most. The site of Jamal in the flesh after so many years sent chills down Jessica's body, followed by a warm tingly sensation and orgasmic river between her legs. Dee saw the look and reaction on Jessica's face and made him feel some type of way. He knew that Jamal still had a hold on her. He could never understand how after so many years she still felt for this nigga.

"Welcome home blood." Dee said to himself, under his breath gritting his teeth like a mad man. They both watched as Jamal turned around and walked back to his momma's house. Dee started the escalade, popped in his Big June CD, and drove off, but not before making mental note that his ex homeboy and good friend J-Bone might be a mutha fuckin problem. A problem that had ta be dealt with quickly. The future of his relationship with Jessica depended on it.

4 GOTTA DO WHAT A MAN GOTTA DO

It had been 6 months and still no job for Jamal. He had applied everywhere but no one was trying to hire an ex-convict convicted for armed robbery. When Jamal seriously thought about what he looked like on paper, he couldn't blame them.

On paper he looked like a monster. And to a certain degree he was, but only if you pushed his buttons. That was J-Bone, this was Jamal, but now Jamal was starting to get frustrated and J-Bone had been occupying his thought process lately.

Jamal was ready to say fuck it and go back to doing what he did best, laying mutha fuckas down for his crown. He got a rush when he hit a nigga off for a big lick. One lick a have you straight for months. The town was full of victims, too. In Jamal's eyes, any and all cross town niggas could get it. Excluding nobody and that went for Mexicans, too. Especially Mexicans. If you wasn't from Skyline Piru, then you could get it. Jamal shook the negative thoughts from his mind as he sat up on his bed, got up and looked in the mirror. When he looked into the mirror, he didn't like the man he saw looking back. He tried to do right, he tried to walk the straight and narrow but that shit got him no where but still here, at his momma's house. Naw, it was time for a change. It was time to put Jamal to bed and welcome...THE RETURN OF J-BONE.

XXX

"Sup wit it Ru, I got that shit you asked me for." Dee spoke into the phone. The person on the other end confirmed like he knew what

Dee was talking about. "That shit" was five pounds of grade A top shelf weed. Dee had just hit a lick the night before at a local dispensary. Him and two young Skyline homies came in through a back door, ski masked and blacked up with bullet proof vests and assault rifles. At first, the workers thought they were being raided, until the very realization kicked in that they were being robbed.

Dee and the other two bloods made everyone walk into the same room, guns drawn. They then removed them of their cellphones and locked them in as they cleaned out the place so now Dee was sitting on a treasure chest of weed and weed items. From top shelf smoke to extra strength edibles. You name it, he had it, and now he was trying to move it.

"A'ight bloodhound, gimme like 3 hours and I should be there," Dee confirmed the time he would arrive with the weed and hung up the phone to start his prosperous day. Just as he went to get dressed, his cellphone went off. The beautiful hood vixen that flashed before the smart phone's screen revealed that it was

Jessica. Dee answered. "Hey hey babygirl."

"Hi, I was calling to see if you was gonna drop me off some money today so I could go shopping." *Damn, straight to the point, huh?* Dee thought to himself. But he knew the business. He knew the only reason he had Jessica was because he kept her pockets laced. And he had no problem with it. Hey, it ain't trickin if you got it right? **Bullshit!** But that was how he saw it. And so did Jessica. She felt like if she was going to be giving it up to another man other than Jamal, then he was gonna pay like the California Lottery.

"Yeah I got you, but you're gonna have ta wait a few hours. I have some business to conduct first," Dee answered Jessica's question.

"Well how long? Because I wanna make it to Saks before they close."

"When I get there! Now quit acting like a money hungry jump off and chillax. Soon as I'm done handling this business, I'll come swoop you up personally and take you shopping." That was even better. That was music to Jessica's ears because with him there, she could convince him to spend even more money. Especially after she gave him head in the dressing room. She almost let him cum in her mouth when he promised to buy the four Donna Karan and Stella McCartney dresses if she did the last time they went shopping. Almost, but not so. So that day she walked out with two pair of Prada's and a matching purse. Still not a bad lick. Let's see what she can get him for today. "Okay Daddy, sorry." Jessica softened up.

"Oh now I'm Daddy, huh?" Dee laughed at how quick Jessica switched it up and got some get right.

"You know how I feel about you," Jessica responded.

"Yep, I sure do," Dee said back sarcastically but at the same time very serious. "Well let me hit you back when I'm on my way ta see you babygirl."

"Okay Daddy, see you soon."

"Yep...soon as I get there."

"TICK! Dadd..." **CLICK!** He hung up the phone laughing as she was talking in mid sentence.

XXX

"Blood, wuss up wit a lick, you still got that other one you was talking to me bout not too long ago?" J-Bone asked his homie Killa.

"Hell yeah Ru! That nigga still out there in PB serving. I actually talked to him yesterday. He told me that he was waiting on a big shipment and that he should be really on deck by tonight."

"Is that right? Wuss blood's name?"

"He call himself Factor. It's ironic, though, because that's what the nigga ain't."

"Well I wouldn't give a fuck if he was at this point. Unless he was a factor from Skyline and since I don't know the nigga, a factor is what he's not. So gimme the full run down on this nigga so we can lay his ass down."

"Fa sho!" Killa responded, with great joy and anticipation for what was yet to come. Killa had been waiting for this moment since the day he was aware of J-Bone's release. He knew that it would only be a matter of time before J-Bone fell back into his old ways and when he did, he wanted to be the first person to put down a lick with him because he knew how J-Bone got down.

Blood was a legend in the set for some of the robberies that he pulled. It's really amazing he's still alive today to talk about it, let alone do it again like he never left. A lot of people wanted his head.They just didn't know it was "his" head they wanted because he would always be smart enough to have his face covered if he jacked you directly, and to stage a jack like he was the one being robbed and set up when doing so indirectly.

J-Bone was hella smart and crafty when it came to that strong arm robbery. Every piece of the puzzle was carefully thought out and meticulously planned. Prison was not an option. Before he went back to jail again he would hold court in the streets. This he would say and this he meant. He would shoot it out with the cops before giving up willingly so Killa sat down and told J-Bone everything he knew about "Factor," the so called homie from Skyline who sold drugs in PB.

XXX

"Wuss up blood, I'm leaving the house now. I should be there in like 20 minutes." Dee said to the homie on the other end of the phone he was taking the five pounds of weed to.

"Alright Ru, P you when you get here." They both hung up and Dee proceeded on his way. He left the house and jumped in his box Chevy on 26's, beating up the block like King Kong in the trunk. Total situation made no sense, seeing how he had five pounds of dank in a Louie bag sitting in the trunk of the most flashiest car in San Diego, headed for the whitest part of SD to sell weed.

Smart! But Dee didn't give a fuck. That's how he did shit. He was ghetto through and through and all the money in the world wasn't gonna change that. He'd have $5,000 in his pockets with some Chuck Taylors and Dickies on. He didn't give a fuck about all that high end over priced shit. You would never catch him in a pair of Gucci or Louie's. Nah, he saved that for the bitch. He'd buy her that shit all day cause that's what she asked for, but when it came to himself, he kept it all the way gangsta.

Dee arrived at the small house in PB not too far from the beach, took the duffle bag out the trunk and walked to the front door. Dee rang the bell as a person opened the door simultaneously as if they psychically knew that Dee was there.

"Wuss up blood? I saw you pull in." *That explains him opening the door so suddenly before I even had a chance to ring the doorbell good,* Dee thought to himself.

"Wuss up Factor? I don't need to lock my doors, do I?" Dee asked, looking back at his Chevy, realizing he forgot to lock his doors.

"Nigga, you in PB, not South East. Yo shit straight. Everybody knows me around here. They ain't finna fuck wit yo shit," Factor responded.

"Well if something happens to my ride, I'm a blame you Ru."

"Well then I suggest you go lock your doors then." They both laughed as Dee did just that before heading back inside to take care of business. He gave the pounds of weed to Factor for $15,000 on consignment, which was love because this was that loud! He could have shipped it to the homies in the ATL and got double the price easy, but then he would have had to worry about packaging and shipping which could be a headache if the package got intercepted and never made it.

So he went with the less greedy safe route, and sold it local. Not to mention, any and everything was profit because he stole the weed. Wasn't like he had his own hard earned money invested or like he grew the weed from scratch and had to wait three to six months to finally see some dough. No no, this was all profit. Tax free money. So Dee dealt with it as such.

"So how's business, you still the man out here on these beaches?"

"Blood, you know I got PB sold the fuck up like a corpse before his funeral," Factor said, trying to sound cool.

"Nigga that shit was corny, if you don't stop tryna sound bool and knock it off."

"Blood I got mouthpiece, you know my Daddy was a pimp."

"Key words...your Daddy! You on the other hand, is a sucka for love when it come ta the pussy!"

"Ah, you just a hater," Factor responded, as they both laughed it off playfully, finished up their business and concluded the meeting.

XXX

"Girl wuss up wit the club tonight? I'm tryna get out and do something," Jessica spoke into the phone to her homegirl Tracy as she laid across her bed. Tracy was Jessica's best friend. They did everything together. Straight partners in crime.

"Girl the club is straight bo bo. Don't be nobody in that bitch but the same old broke niggas acting like they're ballin."

"Yeah you right. It just been a while so I forgot. You know how it is when you haven't been some place in a while, you forget about all the bad things that turned you off about the place until you go back and get a quick reality check," Jessica spoke as she picked up her TV remote and turned the TV on to last night's episode of Love and Hip Hop Atlanta.

"Girl, Stevie J is a straight trick!" Jessica

said, as she watched the episode where Stevie J bought his baby momma a brand new BMW even though they weren't together anymore and she was currently dating someone else.

"Girl you ain't never lied," Tracy responded back. "I wish that nigga was my baby daddy. I'd take that nigga to the bank."

"You and me both girl," Jessica responded and laughed, as she lit a leftover piece of blunt that was sitting in her ashtray off to the side on her nightstand. "Well, I need to find something to do. I'm bored as hell and I'm not trying to be sitting up in the house tonight. Dee suppose ta come over later and take me shopping but ain't no telling when that niggas gonna get here," Jessica said, as she took a final hit of the weed and finished up the doobie.

"Well, the homies are throwing a function at Mission Beach today. But you already know how that's gonna be."

"Yep, a bunch of gangbangers and set rats trying to get put on and seek attention. I'm cool on that," Jessica responded.

"Speaking of which, I forgot to tell you, I

saw J-Bone the other day." The sound of Jessica's ex and first love's name being spoken sent chills down her spine and goosebumps all over her body.

"Girl it's funny you should say that because I saw him as well not too long ago at Skyline Park." Jessica said to her friend, who was on the other end in shock like a fugitive on the run getting caught by the cops.

"What!? And you didn't tell me?"

"Sorry girl, but I've been going through so much lately that it totally slipped my mind. (She lied.) I actually forgot I saw him." (She lied again.) That was the furthest from the truth. She really hadn't been able to get J-Bone out of her head since she saw him a few weeks back while sitting in the parked car giving Dee some head.

"Well, he was looking good. All swole and shit, with that fresh out of prison swag." Jessica thought back to how good J-Bone looked that day as her friend spoke that image into existence.

"Yea well, I don't fuck wit that nigga like dat no more."

"What that gotta do wit how he look?" Tracy responded.

"Girl you know what I mean, quit playing." They both laughed as Jessica playfully scolded.

"Well girl, let me get off this phone and get ready for this nigga Dee to come over and take me shopping."

"Okay girl, I'll call you a little later if I find out about anything going on tonight," Tracy said.

"Alright. If not, we can always fuck with the Gaslamp. You know it's always poppin downtown on a Saturday night."

"Yeah you right. Well hit me up tonight girl around nine and we'll figure it out."

"Okay, will do," Tracy agreed, said her goodbyes and hung up the phone.

XXX

"Alright blood, here's the rundown. The nigga live off Grand Ave. in PB right here, down the street from the beach and 7-11." Killa spoke as he pointed at a Google map image of Factor's house to J-Bone.

"Okay, so how many people inside the house?" J–Bone asked.

"Just him. That's the sweet part. We should be in and out, easy as pie."

"Nigga you ever baked a pie?"

"Huh?" Killa asked with a confused look on his face, not understanding the meaning behind J–Bone's question. "Meaning shit ain't always as easy as it seems. Do he got any guns in the house?" J–Bone asked.

"I know he has a shot gun he keeps by the door."

"Okay good ta know. See that's the type of stuff I'm talking about. We go running up in there half cocked and get our fuckin head blown off."

"You right blood. That's why you the master of this shit. I'm just tryna get in where I fit in," Killa said, then continued to speak. "There's only one way in because his back door is boarded up from the inside. I guess to protect him from intruders."

"Well, that ain't gonna protect shit but us, cause now he can't run out the back when we hit from the front. That also leaves only one door to watch instead of several. That's perfect for a two man lick," J-Bone said as he spoke and thought at the same time.

"I know Ru, that's what I was telling you. Plus blood's a fuckin busta so he ain't finna bust a grape and no one's gonna give a damn when they find out he's been jacked, except his customers who won't have shit to buy the next day because we took it all."

"Yeah dat! So what we gonna do is hit this nigga soon as the sun go down. That way it won't be so late that noise is traveling, nor is it so early that the sun is up, hella bright and putting us on blast."

J-Bone spoke like a commander getting ready for battle. "We gonna try and catch him by surprise and slippin, so we gonna use the 'act like we already know each other tactic. We're gonna knock on the door and ask for him by name. This will make him feel comfortable enough to open the door. After he does, I'm a have that thang thang in his grill quicker than you can say get him. After we force our way inside, we gonna tie the nigga up and blindfold him, after which we gonna take that nigga for everything he has."

"Hell yeah nigga, sounds like a plan to me. A good plan!" Killa responded.

"What, you thought it wasn't what it was? Blood I do this shit for bread n meat. If I don't get em, I don't eat. Failure is not an option but death is. Meaning, if something goes wrong or not as planned, it's either me or him cause I ain't going back to prison blood. Next time my back's up against the wall, we holding court in the streets," J-Bone said with all sincerity. He was done with prison. He wasn't built for that shit. Not physically, but mentally. He knew he didn't have another bid in him, but he also knew that he couldn't stand being broke. You put a hungry man in the room with another civilized but hungry man and leave them there, eventually they're gonna get savaged and eat each other. Same with the streets. Niggas out there hungry so niggas doing what ever they have to do to survive and eat. J-Bone picked up his all black Mausberg pump shotgun off the table, cocked it back and said, "Tonight, it's going down!"

XXX

"Wuss up babygirl, you ready to go shopping?" Dee asked, as he spoke into his iPhone while driving down the 8 East freeway towards Jessica's house. She told him she was ready and waiting on him. Dee arrived at her house 15 minutes later and picked her up. They went to Sak's and spent about $3,500 on high-end clothes and shoes. Jessica was expensive to upkeep like a Kentucky Derby racehorse. Dee didn't mind tricking his...I mean spending his money on her because he knew if he hadn't, she wouldn't have been around longer than two seconds, so he did what he had to and that was kept that pocket book laced!

XXX

KNOCK! KNOCK! KNOCK! J-Bone tapped on the door lightly and waited for a response as he ducked and stood just below the peephole.

"Who is it?" Factor asked, as he approached his front door to see who was knocking on the other side.

"Wuss up blood? It's Bo, quit acting like you don't know who this is Factor and open the door blood for your real homie." J-Bone knew that it was so many niggas from Skyline with Bo at the end of their names that if he said, "Bo" was on the other end of the door, Factor would more than likely believe it was a valid homie.

He also banked on the fact that Factor was a busta. Knowing Factor probably didn't know anybody named "Bo" and should have questioned whoever was at the door like any "real" nigga would've, J-Bone banked on Factor doing the opposite. Not one to come across looking like a busta for not knowing a real homie from Skyline when he saw or heard one, he knew Factor would open the door. And he did just that. Factor opened the door to find a black shotgun barrel in his face and two people blacked up with ski masks on.

"Who the fuc..." The rest of the word and sentence never got a chance to leave Factor's mouth. J-Bone smacked him on the side of his head with the barrel of the shotgun and forced his way in as Killa followed suit.

"Tie that nigga up cuzz." That was the old banana in the tailpipe. J-Bone always used that method to throw his victims off. That way afterwards, they'd think they got took by some crips and would be looking that way for retaliation instead of his, because he was a blood, so there was no way he could have done it. Yeah right, but it always worked. It also helped him sometimes be able to rob the same person multiple times because they never had a clue it was J-Bone that got em.

"Alight loc," Killa responded and went to tie Factor up with the silver duct tape he had in his hands. To their surprise, Factor tried to fight back and threw a sloppy right hook that grazed Killa by inches, so close that he could smell the hairs on his knuckles. J-Bone reacted instantly with the butt of his shotgun, introducing the weapon to the side of Factor's face in holy matrimony. **SMACK!** The hit put Factor on his back as he grabbed his head and yelled out in pain like a wounded animal.

"Shut the fuck up cuzz before I kill your slob ass. Try some shit like that again and

Imma put two slugs in your bitch ass. That's on the hood, loco. Now try me cuzz!" J-Bone spoke and directed Killa to go back to the task at hand, which was tying Factor up so he didn't try nothing else dumb.

Killa tied up his hands first, followed by his feet and mouth, but not before making Factor tell them where all his guns, drugs and money was. At first Factor tried to play stupid like he didn't know what they were talking about in reference to drugs and money. And as far as guns, the only one he owned, was the useless shotgun at the front door that did him no good because he wasn't smart enough to have had it in his hands when he answered the door.

After a couple of stiff kicks to his stomach and mid-section from the two assailants, he quickly regained his thought process and conveniently remembered where the drugs and money was hidden. "There's five pounds of weed in the fridge. The money's under my mattress in the bedroom." Funny how niggas always like to stash their money in a hole under the mattress. That spot is old and hella played out. Even if he had not of told them where his stash was, they would have found it there.

"Thank you for saving us the pleasure of beating you further," J-Bone said to Factor as he reached down and put the tape back over his eyes and lips. The complete darkness and lack of use of his senses caused Factor to panic. He didn't wanna die. Not like this. He knew he wasn't really bout that life. That's why he moved to PB and gang banged out there, because he knew real homies rarely went to the beach and the locals wouldn't question him. They would just take his word for what it was.

What the hell did surfers and college chicks know about gang banging? Not a got damn thing. And that was why Factor moved there. Away from the true gritty side of SD, South East San Diego, where the real gangsters dwelled. Factor didn't want no parts of that. But oh well, too late for all of that because J-Bone was bringing South East to his front door. Gangster shit was going down right there in his living room. He just prayed to God that he made it out of this situation alive. He knew fucking with Daygo niggas it was a 50/50 chance. Not as grimy as L.A. niggas, but still very much with the business. A youngster will have your head in a heartbeat, get caught slipping at the wrong time and place. So knowing all this had Factor shaking like a puss in boots.

"Ahhh there, there. Pull yourself together. This will all be over soon." J-Bone said, while lightly tapping Factor on the side of the face as he said, "there there," after noticing how shook up he was. Killa threw the weed and money in a black duffle bag and alerted J-Bone that everything was all good and they could go.

"You got the shit?" J-Bone asked.

"Yeah, let's go J-Bone, I got it." The sound of J-Bone hearing Killa slip up and say his name in the heat of the moment instantly pissed him off, as he knew he had to now kill Factor. There was no way he could let him live. He heard his name. Killa immediately knew he fucked up the second the words left his mouth. And the look on J-Bone's face confirmed it. Even with the ski mask on, his eyes said it all. **"Shhit!"** Killa said in disappointment.

"Guess this is what I get for fuckin wit amateurs. Thank Killa for getting the chance to meet Jesus a little earlier than expected." J-Bone said, as he walked over towards Factor, shotgun in hand.

"No, no, I don't wanna meet Jesus." Factor said through muffled cries. J-Bone raised the one eyed beast that could strike fear in a Catholic Priest and said, "Sorry blood, nothing personal." **BOOM!** And shot him. J-bone turned, looked Killa in the face with disappointment and said, "Come on blood, let's get the fuck out of here!" Killa looked out the window to make sure the coast was clear, gave J-Bone the signal it was, and disappeared into the night like Batman and Robin.

XXX

"Ooh yeah, fuck this **pussy!**" Jessica screamed out in a heat of passion, as Dee slid up against her side walls with his 9 inch throbbing penis. She could feel the veins rubbing on her clit with every stroke, bringing her to climax every 15 seconds. Jessica had that wet wet and prided herself on it. She also did Kegel exercises to keep her pussy tight.

"Damn babygirl, gimme that pussy! Yeah, let me see you back that ass up!" Dee turned Jessica over and smacked her on the ass as he hit it from the back. Jessica had that suction cup pussy, so every time Dee pulled back, the inside lining of her pussy could be seen gripping the shaft of his penis like elastic.

Jessica moaned and bucked back like a stallion in a rodeo. She rotated her hips in small circles like a professional fuck artist. She reached under her legs searching for that little pink pleasure button that can bring a grown woman to her knees quicker than a Muslim during Salaam.

She found what she was looking for, as she placed her middle finger in her mouth to get it wet and back down towards her lustful center, where her vagina was impatiently waiting to be touched by her gentle fingers. She played with her clit as it grew in size to her stimulating touch. Dee continued fucking her from behind at a steady pace like a jockey trying to win a horse race. He smacked her on the ass with just enough pain to give her pleasure as he pulled her hair. Jessica grabbed ahold of Dee's hands and placed it around her neck. Dee understood what that meant all too well and proceeded to give her what she wanted. He firmly gripped his hands around Jessica's neck like he was trying to choke her from behind and did just that. Choked the shit out of her as he was fucking and ramming her sweet pink pleasure box from behind.

That shit turned Jessica on as she started to cum again for the umpteenth time. Only difference this time was that Dee was cumming as well. There's no better feeling than a man and woman reaching climax together. Dee wrapped his arms under Jessica's body and gripped her tight as he let out his man juice into her tight pink cave of seduction. His body tensed up, toes curled and eyes rolled till the last drop of cum was released from his dick, after which he rolled over onto his back, caught his breath and grabbed the remote off the nightstand as Jessica fell into a coma like sleep.

Breaking news. We're outside 1555 Grand Ave where apparently a man has been shot and killed in his apartment. Neighbors say they heard a fire cracker like bang earlier around 10 p.m. but thought nothing of it. They just summed it up as someone letting off fireworks. Well, needless to say they were not fireworks and a man has lost his life tonight. No word on the motive or suspects at this time. The name of the victim is being withheld until family can be notified of his death.

Dee just stood there holding the remote, staring at the TV screen in disbelief. He was watching the very house he was just at earlier, now on the 11 o'clock news, yellow taped up with a body being removed. He couldn't help but think about his weed.

"**Shit!** What the fuck happened?" Dee asked himself. He then turned off the TV and put his clothes on. "Yo Jessica, wake up! I gotta run."

"Where you going baby, it's late."

"Look woman, I said I gotta go. I ain't got

time to be doing no talking right now." He kissed her on the forehead and said, "I'll be back," as he ran out the house to see what the word on the streets was, get more info and find out exactly what had happened and who was responsible.

XXX

J–Bone and Killa ran up the stairs to their trap house on Imperial where they usually served smokers, rushed inside, and closed the door.

"Blood, you's a dumb mutha fucka! How the fuck you gone say my real name during a robbery? I thought you was smarter than that," J–Bone said to Killa, hella upset behind the fact that he had to turn a simple robbery into a full fledge murder.

"I know. I fucked up homie. I was just caught up in the moment and slipped."

"Nigga, slippin gets you caught up. One slip could land you behind bars doing a life sentence. The prison yard is full of mutha fuckas that 'just slipped.' Blood, you gotta be sharper than that Ru," J-Bone explained to Killa.

"I know blood. It won't happen again."

"Well, let's go see what we got and count this money up," J-Bone instructed, as he took his ski mask off and threw the shotgun on the couch. They counted up the money first, which came out to a little over $20,000. Not bad for a two man lick. They weighed out and divided the drugs. Along with the 5 pounds of Dee's weed, they had came up on 200 molly pills, 3 ounces of meth and some shrooms. The shrooms would be harder for them to move because of the type of circle they hung with. Shrooms was more of a happy, party, club kid type of drug. Not too many Southeast niggas was getting high off shrooms, but come with some weed, speed, coke, or PCP and it's on. You'd be lucky to last the night with your supply.

So all in all, good lick! J-Bone was more than pleased with the outcome. Other than the murder, everything went just as planned. Now it was time to get his shit together. Even though that situation turned out to be a good lick, J-Bone was more than realistic with himself and knew that it still wouldn't be enough to sustain, but more or so get him started. And that's exactly what it did.

5 DRAMA

It had been 2 weeks since the ordeal that took place between J-Bone, Killa and Factor. Word on the streets was that he owed the Mexican mafia some money and they came to collect and killed him for it. That was a very ridiculous explanation and assumption though. Because everyone knows that, the Mexican mafia doesn't fuck with niggas.

J-Bone was laying low stacking his money and only buying what was needed. The smart thing to do after a high profile robbery, or any robbery for that matter. But Killa was doing the opposite. He was rolling around the hood flossing in a candy painted box Chevy on 26's with Gucci interior. He went from no car to rolling like an episode of Pimp My Ride.

Killa was bringing a lot of attention to himself, especially to those that really knew him and what he was about. Like the homies from the set. They all grew up together and Killa was never the baller type, so him sitting in this box Chevy that looked like it should be featured in a dirty south video, had him looking really out of place.

"Blood, wuss brackin Ru?" Killa said, as he pulled into the Moonlight Liquor Store's parking lot where the homie Big June was standing chilling posted up, waiting on a ride to the studio.

"Oh wuss up wit it Ru, this you?" June said, pointing at Killa's car.

"Yea Dat! I just got it Saturday."

"Blood this mutha fuckas bick. What you do, hit the lottery?"

"Something like that," Killa said, then laughed it off.

"Well I see ya boy. I was waiting on the

homie $ki.Bo to pick me up, so I could go to the studio and lay these tracks. You know I'm fresh out and thirsty like a nigga trapped in the desert with no water."

"How long you been out?" Killa asked.

"Shit, not even 3 weeks. Right around the time when that shit happened to Factor. You heard about that shit right?"

"Yeah, but he wasn't no factor..." Big June cut him off.

"So what! He was a homie from the turf, representing the same thing as you and I. I ain't with all this new 2013 shit with homies being divided and internal beef amongst the Set. That shit is bad for business. I love all bloods and homies that represent this P-Funk!"

"Well I hate to say it Ru, but times have changed. The rolling 80's and 90's are long gone. It's a different breed and era out here blood," Killa responded.

"I guess it is. So what you got up right now, can you take me to the studio? I'm trying to get up out the set before gang detail catch me slippin and I catch a violation on some bullshit," June asked.

"Oh I got you Ru, come on. I'll take you, where's it at?"

"The Bat Cave," June responded, like Killa should know exactly what and where he was talking about going after saying the name. The Bat Cave was a known studio in Daygo that a lot of local artists use to record their music. It was one of the best studios in San Diego for recording hip hop.

"Hop inside," Killa said, as he grabbed some miscellaneous papers and things that were lying on his front seat and threw them in the back. Big June opened the car door and got inside as they headed for the studio.

"So what else you hear about what happened to Factor?" Killa asked, as they drove down to the studio, inquiring to see just how much June knew. "Hell I don't know much, but I know it ain't what people are saying. And that's that the Mexican Mafia did it. I can bet my right nut they ain't had shit to do with it."

"How you know that?" Killa asked.

"Because I just got out of the pen with nothing but Surenos (Mexican mafia) and they don't fuck with niggas like that," June answered his question as he noticed the nervous and puzzled look on Killa's face due to June's response. "Why you ask?"

"No reason, just wondering if you heard anything new or different, but that's the same thing I heard so I guess not.""

"Well, I'm a strong believer in what happens in the dark always comes to light Ru. So I'm sure the real story on what happened will come out eventually. It always does," June said, as they merged on to the freeway and headed to the Bat Cave.

XXX

Dee was pacing back n forth talking on the phone to one of the homies. "Blood, that loss I took a couple weeks back really hurt me gangsta. I had a lot riding on them 4 pounds. I been spending a lot of money, haven't been putting away as much as I should have, and now I'm paying the price for that shit."

In just 2 weeks time, things had taken a dramatic turn and flipped like a cheerleader in competition fighting for first place. Since Dee had stood to make almost $20,000 on the weed that J-Bone had jacked from Factor and now he couldn't, his pockets was feeling the hit tremendously. $20,000 might not be a whole lot for a super kingpin type baller, but for an average street hustler from the ghetto trying to make it, $20,000 is like $200,000. A nigga with $20 grand will feel like he's hood rich and made it. Now Dee wasn't broke by any means. That wasn't the problem. The problem was that he spent more money than he saved. That, and the fact that he had Jessica who had expensive taste. And he knew that if he wanted to keep her, then he would have to maintain the level of living she was accustomed to.

"Blood hold on a second, my line beeping." Dee spoke into the phone as he switched over and greeted the caller. "Hello, may I help you?" Dee asked sounding square as a box answering the phone in his white voice. The person on the other end laughed as he got thrown off, but then got serious as he informed Dee of some serious news.

It was one of the young homies from the set. Dee listened to what the homie had to say as his facial expression grew angry. Dee gritted his teeth like a tweeker on a good one. He curled his top lip in the right side corner of his face like Elvis before saying, "Is that right? Okay blood, check it out, round up the squad and meet me at Red Blood's spot. Bring them thang thangs, cause we gonna let them thangs rang tonight!" The person on the other end agreed, hung up the phone, and went to do as Dee ordered. Dee hung up the phone as well...with the back of the wall!

XXX

The streets had been talking and word had gotten out that J-Bone and Killa was behind the robbery and murder of Factor. Apparently,

Killa's dumb ass was laid up one day popping mollies with some chick from the Set, and spilled it all pillow talking. A lot of men's downfalls have been behind pillow talking with a woman. And it was beginning to look like Killa's would be no different. That's what that call was about that Dee had gotten earlier. Apparently, the chick that Killa was messing with, was also messing around with three other homies from the set and told them what Killa had told her.

Two didn't care because they were a couple of real reputables and light weight liked the fact that Factor had gotten jacked. But the other homie saw things how June saw it, which was, If you represent the same thing he represented, then you was bool with him. He had love for "all" bloods and that went double if you was from the set. So once he got news of the treachery, he spread it throughout the set quicker than a forest fire in a dry brush in southern California.

XXX

"Blood I don't give a fuck who knows we jacked him! That nigga was a busta...**period!**"

"Nigga you sound stupid!" J-Bone said to Killa, then continued. "That's not the fuckin point Ru. The fact that the streets know about it is. How long you think before the popo does, too?" That got Killa's attention. "Yea nigga, ain't no statue of limitation on murder! You fuckin wit our future."

"Blood I understand where you're coming from...I fucked up." Killa said, with his head down towards the floor like a puppy that'd just been scolded.

"Fuck it blood, ain't nothing we can do about it now. But word on the streets is Dee looking for some type of get back..." Killa cut J-Bone off in mid sentence. "Why Dee give a fuck about what happened to Factor?"

"Apparently some of that weed we took from that nigga belonged to Dee. Factor was selling it for him."

"Damn Ru, is that right, what's the chance in that?" Killa responded. J-Bone continued, "Me personally, I don't give a fuck! Dee violated our trust and friendship when he fucked with my bitch Jessica. So at this point in time, I could care less about jackin that nigga's shit. Actually, payback's a bitch. He got the hoe and I got the doe. Fair exchange ain't no robbery." J-Bone shrugged it off as such.

"Shit, well I feel the same way to a fault. I mean Dee is still the homie when it comes to me but if blood is feeling some type of way about me for indirectly jackin him for his work, then we can handle biz however he sees fit," Killa said, as bullets rang out from outside and through the front window facing the street of J-Bone's mother's house. Killa and J-Bone quickly hit the floor like they just spotted the second coming of Jesus and covered their heads as broken shards of glass littered the room. **BOOM BOOM BOOM!!! DOO DOO DOO DOO DOO!!!** The semi automatic gun fire kept up for what seemed like forever until the clips were empty. The sound of a car screeching off could be heard as J-Bone and Killa lied on the floor in shock and anger.

"Blood you alright?" J-Bone called out to

Killa. "Yeah I'm bool blood. Just cut my hands a little from the glass on the floor."

"Alright blood, that's how they wanna play it?" J-Bone said to no one in particular as he got up off the floor madder than King Kong on top of the empire state building. "Just gonna disrespect my momma's house and shoot it up huh?" Luckily J-Bone's mother wasn't home at the time. She had just left not even 5 minutes prior to go food shopping and run errands.

"Alright blood, these niggas wanna go to war." J-Bone said out loud as he pulled himself together and thought about how he was gonna retaliate.

"Blood, these niggas must be ready to die to bring funk to your momma's house!" Killa said. "I'm ready for whatever my nigga. Set or no set, it's anybody killa wit me. Fuck boy come at me the wrong way and gonna find 8 slugs in his back."

"Yea Dat!" J-Bone agreed, as he calmed his nerves, got on his cellphone and called a few Skyline young heavy hitters. Niggas that was really bout that murder game and still fucked with J-Bone, despite him jacking and killing Factor. This was the half who agreed with J-Bone, which was that Factor was a busta and had it coming. Once news got out about what happened to Factor, how he got robbed and killed and who was behind it, the Set got divided so half the homies was on J-Bone's side and the other half was on Dee's side.

J-Bone lived near Skyline Park which was considered the "TOPS." Dee lived closer to Moras High School which was considered the "BOTTOMS." Unfortunately, this made it easy for niggas to choose sides and pledge their allegiance. The TOPS ran with J-Bone and the BOTTOMS ran with Dee. Just that simple. J-Bone hung up the phone and cleaned up the aftermath of the failed hit before his mother came home. Little did he know that it wasn't a hit but a message. A message from Dee that he declared war and nothing was off limits. Not even his mother.

XXX

"Blood, we shot that nigga's house up just like you told us to." A young Skyline soldier reported back to Dee.

"Anyone get hit?" Dee asked.

"I don't think so, we just shot up the window as we saw him and that nigga Killa drop to the floor."

"Alright, good shit! I wanna give him a chance to respond to my message. Bring back my money or prepare yourself for war." Dee sat back in his leather office chair like a boss and lit a blunt. He was laid up in a warehouse somewhere in the cut, surrounded by about 20 Skyline Gangsters in a secluded location. Dee had read The Art Of War and knew that posting up in the set like a sitting duck and waiting on J-Bone to retaliate would be foolish.

He also knew that he could've just caught J-Bone and Killa slipping and killed them both, but he wanted them to suffer. Not only that, but he wanted his work back. He also didn't like the way they did Factor. So with all that in mind, he felt the need to make J-Bone pay in a major way. He was making it seem like if J-

Bone repaid him for the weed he took, then everything would be fine. But that was all cap (bullshit). Dee had no intentions on letting J-Bone live.

XXX

"Hello," Jessica answered her iPhone.

"Girl have you heard the latest?" The voice excitedly said on the other end before even a simple hello.

"Who's this, Tracy?" Jessica asked.

"Yeah girl, the streets is buzzing about your man and your ex. Apparently, J-Bone had something to do with that hit on Factor and Dee is salty about it because some of that work they got belonged to Dee. I guess Factor was slanging it for him. Now Dee and J-Bone is at each other's head. I hear it's on, on site." Bitches always seemed to know about the latest hood gossip. They were considered the ghetto CNN. Who needed the nightly news when you had local hood rats to report to and keep you informed? Jessica was stunned by the news.

"Get the fuck outta here, you serious?" Jessica responded.

"If I'm lying I'm dying and I look too good to go just yet," Tracy retorted. Tracy continued giving Jessica the details of all that she had heard about the robbery/homicide and riff between Dee and J-Bone. Once done, Jessica immediately hung up and called Dee's cell but got no answer and sent straight to voicemail. She hung up, grabbed her bag and left the house.

6 I'LL TAKE YOU TO WAR

Bullets rang out as Dee sat eating at a taco shop located on The Four Corners Of Death. The Four Corners was off Imperial Ave and a hotspot for death and niggas slippin. Dee knew better than to be out right now during a war but he got hungry and knew the taco shop on Imperial had the best burritos so he took his chances. That was his first mistake. His second was underestimating the power of J-Bone.

Dee quickly took cover as one of the young homies he was with immediately drew his gun and started letting off in the direction of the gunfire. Two innocent church ladies walking across the street got hit and killed on impact. Dee scurried for cover while simultaneously reaching for his gun. Slippin number two, he left it in the car. **"Shit!"** Dee felt like a sitting duck. All he could do was stay low and pray that the ordeal would be over a lot sooner than later. Pandemonium developed as people ran and took cover fighting to get away to safety. Most made it, some was not so lucky as the Mack-11 spit out the stolen Buick and lit up the taco shop. **Rat-a-tat-tat-tat!**

"Take that mutha fucka!" The young Skyline hit crew known as The Goon Squad yelled out as they rolled by shooting. The Goon Squad was a couple of Skyline hot heads that ran with J-Bone and was serious when it came to putting in work. Nothing and nobody was off limits. Between the crew they had over 50 bodies up under their belt. Make that 51 as 4 bullets caught the nigga Dee was with in the head, neck, leg and torso, sending his body into convulsions as he dropped his gun and hit the ground.

The car skidded off, disappeared and was

gone as quick as it arrived. Dee was safe but his man was dead. Dee looked over to his left, only to find the homie dead, lying in his own blood with his eyes still open. It was an image that Dee would never be able to shake from his mind.

"Blood that nigga J-Bone's bout ta pay with his life!" Dee said, as he hurried to his feet and shook the spot before law enforcement arrived.

Dee jumped in his ride and headed back to the honeycomb hideout. Eight niggas sat playing bones and smoking weed as Dee busted through the door. **"Blood, that nigga got me fucked up!"** Dee spat, looking frantic and stumbling in. **"They killed B-Rock blood!"** B-Rock was the young gunner that was with Dee who caught the four bullets.

"Who killed B-Rock?" One of the eight soldiers sitting at the table asked as he got up reaching for his gun that was lying to the side.

"Who you think? That nigga J-Bone. Who else?" Dee shot back, looking at the young nigga like he was stupid for not using common sense.

"So why we sitting here talking for? Let's strap up and get active," another nigga sitting at the table bellowed. Dee's phone went off and he looked at the screen. He noticed the picture ID. It was Jessica. He didn't have time to talk to her right now so he sent her to voicemail.

"Blood, that's exactly what we're finna do. On the set, that nigga's gonna bleed tonight!" Dee responded, walking to the back room to clean up, assess the situation, and figure out his next plan of attack.

XXX

"Yea blood, we served that nigga!" One of the Goon Squad niggas spat as he spoke on the phone to J-Bone."

"Blood what I tell you about talking on the phone?" J-Bone responded.

"My bad Ru, we on the way back to the spot now. I'll fill you in when we get there."

"No doubt, should of just did that in the first place."

"Yea yea, I know. I wasn't thinking. Nigga

got caught up in the moment. It won't happ...
ah shit!!!" The goon spat, cutting himself off
while looking in the rear view mirror, noticing
that the police was now behind them. The
niggas in the car panicked but tried to remain
calm and avoid suspicion but the cops was
already on them. They got word of the suspect
vehicle involved in the shooting through
numerous eyewitness accounts, not even two
minutes after the shooting occurred.

"What's wrong blood?" J–Bone inquired.

"The popo is behind us and I think we're
about to be pulled over."

"Fuck! Is that right?"

"Hell yea blood, fuck! They just hit the
sirens," the nigga on the phone with J–Bone
and driving the stolen Buick said as he put the
pedal to the metal and gassed the late model
vehicle. Two goons sitting in the back seat
leaned out the back windows and started
firing. One of the bullets shattered the
windshield of the police cruiser. Another bullet
whizzed by missing the policeman sitting in
the passenger seat by inches.

"Pull Over!" The police blared through the

bullhorn as the car full of killers paid them no mind. Now they were in a high speed chase, racing all through the streets of South East San Diego trying to get away.

"Blood we gotta shake these niggas before the ghetto bird (helicopter) get on our ass," one of the niggas in the car spat.

"Blood, tell me about it. What you think I'm trying to do?" The nigga driving responded. They bent a sharp right and flew down Woodman Street towards the Set. The police were still on their tail. They hit a couple side streets trying to lose them and ran over a speed bump doing 60 miles, which sent the Buick airborne like an episode of The Dukes of Hazard. The car swerved side to side as parts from the undercarriage fell off. The police were still on their bumper, literally. They tried to tap the corner of the bumper to send the car out of control and bring the chase to a halt.

The car did just that as it span out of control and hit a light pole.

"Freeze!" The police yelled, as they hopped out of the smoking squad car, guns raised and itching to shoot. The stolen car's doors opened up as The Goon Squad took off running in different directions, guns blazing.

"I said **freeze!**" **Boom boom boom!** The police let off and instantly shot two of the goons before they'd realized what even happened. The bullets slammed one goon up against the stolen Buick as he slid down the side of the car and fell to the floor, gun still in hand.

The other was shot directly in the head, which caused his dome to explode on impact. His lifeless body fell to the ground as well, still twitching from aftershock. The driver and passenger of the stolen vehicle took off running through the back streets of Skyline. By this time, the ghetto bird was up high in the sky searching as well. Once you got the bird locked in on your whereabouts, there was no place to hide. The cops took off on a foot pursuit after the killer assassins.

The sounds of police dogs barking could be heard in the distance as the assailants continued to scale fences and run through backyards trying to get away. Police blocked the area and flooded the streets with San Diego's finest black and whites. One of the assailants ran down an alley, hopped the fence, and entered the backyard of an old couple that lived off 69th Street and entered the house through the backdoor. When he tried the knob, the door opened. The startled couple was sitting in the living room watching TV. The lady screamed out of shock.

"Bitch shut the fuck up before I paint the back of the wall with your brains!" The killer said, waving his pistol in the woman's direction. The woman instantly shut up as her husband held her close while eyeing the intruder. The killer paced back in forth, peeping out the window shades and praying the cops didn't know his whereabouts.

"Come out with your hands up!" was heard through a bullhorn. The intruder ran to the window and peeped out the blinds. When he did, he saw a barrage of law enforcement staring back at him.

"Shit!" He said to himself. "How the fuck did they find me so fast?" He asked out loud to no one in particular. The cops knew his whereabouts because a neighbor who was peeping out their window at the start of the pursuit saw the assailant force himself inside the house next door and called the police.

Now shit was getting real. The reckless killer with no remorse for human life was pacing back and forth in the apartment rubbing his temple with the tip of the barrel of the gun. "Think, think!" He said to himself, but there was nothing to think about. Either he was coming out or they were coming in. He knew how Daygo Police got down. They wouldn't give a fuck about the hostages. If he didn't surrender, they were coming in to get him out. Period! Just that simple. His partner who had taken off running in the opposite direction before he invaded the old couple's home, had been caught by police not even two blocks away. The ghetto bird (Police helicopter) had spotted him and alerted foot patrol and all units.

Just as he was thinking and contemplating his next move, a loud boom and crash was heard as smoke filled the room. The cops had sent a smoke bomb through the front window of the apartment. The effects were instant as the Skyline intruder dropped his gun to the floor and covered his eyes. But it was too late. As he coughed and gasped for air, the front door busted open off the hinges, followed by a dozen or so angry SWAT, guns raised and ready to shoot. Lucky for the intruder they didn't. Daygo Police were known to shoot first and ask questions last with their scary ass.

"Freeze mother fucker!" a cop spat, but the Skyline hardhead wasn't trying to hear it. He blindly reached on the floor for his gun as he slowly regained his eyesight. Jail wasn't an option for the young rida. He knew he had done too much to turn back. Fuck it, he was gonna hold court in the streets, as he placed his hand on the gun that laid dormant on the floor. That would be as close as he got to picking it up and letting off a shot. Needless to say, the SWAT team unleashed a hail of bullets that sent the young man's body twitching, like he was doing the pop lock on Beat Street. When it was all said and done, a young man was dead, surrounded by his own blood as an old couple sat shocked on the couch speechless from what they had just witnessed. Just another day in the South East.

7 FRIENDEMIES

J-Bone and Killa sat back in astonishment as they listened to and watched the breaking news develop right before their eyes on the 55'' inch plasma that hung from the wall. They watched as one of their homies was taken into custody and the other was bum rushed and killed by officers via live TV. J-Bone was in shock. Killa spoke first.

"Blood, that's brazy!"

"Yea, tell me about it. We just lost four soldiers on one mission. No matter how you look at it Blood, that's all bad!" Killa agreed. Shit had hit the fan on both sides and now they were in an all out war. In the next couple of days in the course of a week, both sides had received multiple casualties. Dee would strike and take out one of J-Bone's men. Then J-Bone would strike back and take out two of his. The crazy part about the whole ordeal is that at one point in time they were all friends. All from the same Set. All riding for a common cause. But this new beef between J-Bone and Dee had caused a serious rift in the Set and made many choose sides. Never before in Skyline history had the Tops and Bottoms clicked up and got into it with each other. Yeah there was your occasional fist fight here and there between homies but this was beyond that. Niggas were shooting and killing each other ON SITE! The Set was hella divided and in a frenzy. Six murders had taken place in the course of six days. One murder every 24 hrs. A Tit for Rat-a-Tat-Tat! Old friends were now sworn enemies. Skyline would never be the same.

XXX

J-Bone was walking through the old Fam-Mart shopping center. It was an indoor swap meet. The type you find in every hood across America. Fam-Mart used to be the hood hangout. On any given Sunday the parking lot would be packed with Lowriders and Gang members. Hoodrats and hoes. Hustlers and busters. You name it, they were there. But now Fam-Mart was a fraction of its former self. The owners had raised its rent on the booth renters by so much that more than half was forced to shut down. This caused the place to be 75% empty with just a few booths left selling the bare necessities.

J-Bone went to pick up a few Pro Club tees, and some new music to bump. As he was leaving one of the shops, he bumped smack dap into Jessica, literally, which caused her to drop what she was holding.

"Damn nigga, watch where you…" was all she got out her mouth before she looked up and realized who was standing before her. The look on both their faces said it all. They were both in shock. This was the first time the ex couple had seen each other face to face since

J-Bone's release. Jessica was lost for words, J-Bone wasn't.

"So how you been Jessica? Long time no see." J-Bone spat in a smooth player like voice, showing none of the remorse and anger that he harbored inside towards Jessica. She answered him back.

"Ha...hi Jamal," was all she said in a slight whisper like tone. She could barely look J-Bone in the eyes. She knew she was foul for how she did him while he was in prison. Leaving him for the dead and getting with his best friend. No amount of words could excuse that treachery. It was bad enough that she left him hanging while doing his bid, but then she had to add fuel to the fire by fucking and getting with his homie. Both them mutha fuckas broke the code in J-Bone's eyes.

"So how's life in Jessica's world these days? You know the streets is talking." J-Bone said, speaking in regards about her and Dee.

"Well I can say the same about you," she spat back, with a look on her face like, "Yeah I know wuss up between you and Dee." J-Bone payed it no mind and disregarded her sarcastic response like he never heard her say shit.

"Look, this ain't that and that ain't this, so miss me with that bullshit." J-Bone hissed, with a look on his face that said, "Don't push your luck." Jessica knew to tread lightly and watch her mouth. J-Bone was the type to put a foot in a bitch ass when called for and she knew that she had already done more than enough to have J-Bone pissed enough to go there so she switched gears on him.

"I really missed you," she said seductively, trying to play on his emotions and feelings. Jessica hoped J-Bone still cared for her.

This bitch got some nerve, J-Bone thought to himself, so he played a fool to catch a fool. J-Bone was a Cancer and could hold a grudge like none other when he felt betrayed. He could see in Jessica's eyes that she still had love for him, or maybe it was lust. Whatever it was, J-Bone was gonna use it, as well as her, to get to Dee.

J-Bone softened up his expression and said, "I missed you, too. You were all I thought about while I was doing that bid." J-Bone said with a hint of sarcasm.

"I know I let you down and I'm sorry. I was in a weird place after you got arrested. I felt like my whole world had came crashing down on me."

Is this bitch serious? Let me down...weird place...world came crashing down. **Bitch how the fuck you think I felt!** J-Bone thought to himself as he listened to Jessica's bullshit explanation. She continued.

"I know that may come across as bullshit, but I was really confused after you got locked up and had nowhere to turn. I felt lonely..." J-Bone cut her off in mid sentence.

"Bitch are you serious?" Jessica was in shock to say the least.

"Did you just call me a bitch?"

"You got damn right. That's your bullshit excuse for leaving me for the dead? Because you was lonely you fucked my homie, really? Bitch you don't think I was lonely in that little ass cell wondering if you was ever gonna visit, drop a letter or keep in touch?" Jessica knew he was right. All she could do was drop her head in shame and take J-Bone's verbal assault. She knew she deserved it and a lot more. J-Bone didn't play when it came to his love for Jessica. He once put a man in a coma for six months for touching her butt at a nightclub while she was passing by on her way to the restroom. J-Bone saw the thirsty nigga and his evil grin as he dapped his man to the side for the lustful deed. J-Bone was on the nigga like a pitbull with tunnel vision in a dogfight. He hit him off with two Mayweather jabs to his nose, instantly crushing it on impact that was followed by a slam to the club floor directly on his head which put him in a coma. His boy that was with him didn't want no problems as he put up his hands like someone told him to freeze with a gun drawn during a robbery.

"How the fuck out of all the people on this planet to fuck with, you chose my homeboy? Not just my homeboy, but my so called best friend?"

"I know it doesn't make it right, but when you got locked up, Dee would come by and look after me, make sure I was straight. Mentally and financially he would look out. Eventually one thing led to another and here we are. If I could take it back I would," she lied. Jessica was about her money and the way Dee was tricking it off to keep her, she would have done whatever she needed to do to keep them checks rolling in.

J-Bone was furious but tried not to let it show. Unfortunately, he was a terrible actor because Jessica could see the anger written across his face. She reached for his hand but he pulled away and kept his distance.

"Look babe, I don't know what you take me for, but you know me well enough to know that the moment you fucked my nigga was the moment you created a war. I'll never forget how you did me while I was down. Loyalty goes a long way with me and both of you have proven to be very disloyal. With that being said...in time, I can forgive you."

J-Bone was lying outside of his neck as Jessica's eyes lit up. That was exactly the reaction he wanted. He was playing a sucker to catch a sucker. He knew how much Dee was infatuated with Jessica and felt he could use her to get to him. Man's biggest downfall has always been related to a woman. Shit, if it wasn't for a woman, we'd all be sitting pretty right now letting it all hang out in The Garden Of Eden chilling.

"Really? You can seriously forgive me for what I done?"

"I can forgive, but I won't 'ever' forget"

"I understand. I owe you more than I can ever give or repay. What can I say?"

"Oh I have a way for you to repay." J–Bone said, looking Jessica directly in her eyes with an expression that was serious than a mutha fucka. Jessica didn't like the sound of that. Nor his expression. The tone in his voice let her know that shit was about to get real. She didn't care, though. There was nothing she wouldn't do to get back with J–Bone...Nothing!

XXX

Okay Blood, check this out young rida. Imma need you to find this nigga and bring it to him in a real way. We at war and I won't rest until I have his head on a platter. The nigga is foul for jacking and killing the homie. Shit if he did it to him, what would stop him from doing it to one of us?" Dee spoke to the young Skyline hitter who was known for putting in work.

"I got you big homie. Don't worry about shit. After I'm done with that nigga, he gon wish somebody else had found him. I'm bout ta show you how D-Brown get down!" That was the young hitter's name. D-Brown for "Daygo Brown" paying homage to the old school Padre colors. They called him D.B. for short. D.B. was a crazy street nigga that killed so many people that at 18, his 170 lb frame and unintimidated look still struck the fear of GOD in any and everyone that knew and came across him. He was a real live wire. Had zero regard for life. The perfect gun for hire.

"Alright then Blood, keep me posted." Dee said to the young Skyline homie as he finished up their meeting and lit a blunt, sat back in his leather chair in the office of the warehouse they were stashed at and watched D.B. exit the building with nothing but killing J-Bone on his mind.

XXX

Killa sat at the stoplight on the Four Corners of Death, a known intersection in South East San Diego that got its name from the many murders that occurred there. One must be on point at all times when roaming through the streets of South East, and even more so when posted or spotted on the Four Corners of Death.

Killa sat in his box Chevy bumping the Homie Big $ki.Bo's album "Let Me Pimp Or Let Me Die" when a blue Impala with tinted windows pulled up alongside of him, rolled down their windows and opened fire.

BOOM BOOM BOOM!!! Killa never saw it coming but was quick on the draw after the first shots rang out. He kept his Heat on his lap for times just as such. He instantly ducked down into the seat while simultaneously punching the gas, right through the red light, just missing a semi by inches as he gripped his desert eagle and returned fire.

Now they were in a high speed chase racing down Euclid Ave towards East Daygo, shooting back and forth like some Italian gangsters in an old mob flick. But this was no movie. Killa's back window shattered upon impact as bullets entered the vehicle. Killa knew he was outgunned and had to seek refuge fast! He bent a corner on Market Street headed towards Crip territory, placing Killa in even more danger. But "fuck it" was his thought process, *I'll take my chances.* Killa put the pedal to the metal but the box Chevy was no match for the new Impala. The two cars were now side to side. So close that Killa could make out the driver and the occupants. One of the assailants he recognized from the jump. It was a nigga they called 2-Face from The Bottoms. He was definitely one of Dee's killas.

At that point, one of the gunmen in the back seat took aim while leaning out the window and got to busting! **BOOM BOOM BOOM BOOM!** The last bullet hit Killa's back tire which exploded on impact, sending the car fishtailing out of control and into a pole.

Killa quickly took off his seat belt and exited the smoking vehicle, gun drawn and ready for battle. But Killa was out manned, out gunned and didn't stand a chance. Knowing this, Killa took off on foot down a side street with 2-face and the other assailants not too far behind. Bullets whizzed by Killa's head as they continued busting. Lucky for him, they were a terrible shot. It was like when you saw people shooting a million rounds on TV and no one got hit. Still being, Killa knew it would only be a matter of time and only took "one" bullet to put him on his ass and end this debacle. So Killa hit a quick left down a side alley and hopped the first fence he came across which put him in the yard face to face and nose to nose with a vicious Pitbull. *Fuck, what's the chance?* Killa thought to himself. Just as the dog leaped to attack, Killa quickly aimed his gun and blew off the dog's jaw, instantly killing him on site. Killa got up and continued hopping fences.

2-Face and the car full of hitters trying to kill him rolled up and down the back streets looking for him. After another 5 minutes of not being able to locate him, they gave up and disappeared. Lucky for Killa too, because that last bullet he used on the dog was just that, his last bullet. Killa felt relieved to know that he had survived the attempt on his life, but now he had another issue to deal with. How the fuck he was gonna get out of enemy Crip territory without getting noticed!

XXX

"Uh Uh Uh, oh fuck me Daddy!" You could hear the sounds of passion through the Motel 6 walls as J-Bone fucked the shit out of Jessica. Anger mixed with lust fueled his passion and rage as he took it out on the pussy. There was no love making here. He was fucking with pure aggression. J-Bone was hitting the pussy from the back doggy style. Hands around the back of her neck forcing her face into the pillow. This was all strategic and part of J-Bone's master plan.

After seeing and talking to Jessica for the first time he been home, he made it seem like he forgave her for her treachery. They then got a room in Chula Vista of E. Street at the Motel 6. His plan was to put his dick game down mean, having Jessica feel like all was forgiven, get up in her head and ultimately, have her lead him to Dee.

"Who's pussy is this?" J-Bone said through clenched teeth and long strokes.

"Yours Daddy!" *Yeah right, bet you wasn't saying that when you was fucking Dee!* J-Bone thought to himself as he got angrier and continued to take it out on the pussy. He slid his dick out of Jessica's wet pussy and rammed it straight into her dry ass. She yelled out a scream and jumped forward but couldn't move because of the vise grip clamp J-Bone had around her waist.

"Ahhhh!!!!"

""Shut up all that screaming and take this dick!" J-Bone responded

"I can't Daddy, I can't. Please take it out. It hurts so much!"

"Well now you know how I felt in prison...Like you **'FUCKED'** me. Ain't a good feeling is it?" J-Bone said as he continued fucking the shit out of Jessica's ass to the point it started to bleed.

"I'm sorry Daddy, please take it out, please!" Her cries fell on deaf ears as J-Bone continued to fuck her ass...pun intended. Again, he was teaching her a lesson. One she would never forget. Cries of passion quickly turned into cries of pain as she screamed to the heavens to stop this hellish act that was taken place. As blood started to appear on the shaft of J-Bone's dick from the ripped flesh that his 8 1/2 inch anaconda had caused, he pulled out his dick forcefully as Jessica flopped down on the bed face first crying damn near motionless. J-Bone had gotten his point across. Don't fuck him or get **"FUCKED"** in the process. Again, pun intended. The cold part about it all, J-Bone didn't even allow himself to nut. To do so, he felt would've been a sucker move, and he refused to let this bitch think she could sucker him for a second time. J-Bone spoke.

"Alright, now that we got that out the way... let's talk about what I need you to do."

8 THE BIG PAYBACK

"Blood, park right here." D.B. said to one of the homies who was driving the hot model (stolen car) they were in, pulling up to the curb a few feet away from J-Bone's momma's house. "Cut the lights blood, keep the motor running and wait here." D.B. said, as he opened the door of the stolen Honda Civic and got out.

J-Bone's momma was in the house resting when she heard what she thought to be shattered glass as the sound instantly woke her up out of her sleep. The startled old woman fumbled for her glasses off the night stand and opened the dresser drawer to reveal a small gun safe. She reached for the small set of keys to open the safe that was laying on top of the night stand next to the lamp.

By this point she could hear footsteps aggressively approaching. She stuck the key into the lock on the safe as her room door swung open leaving her face to face with D.B. She tried not to panic and remain calm as she went to turn the key, open the safe and remove the loaded weapon that was inside, all before the assailant made his way over towards her and did whatever he had intentions on doing, which couldn't have been anything good. Unfortunately, she was too slow and D.B. was too fast.

"What you think you doing old bitch?" Said the young nigga with no regard for life, let alone his elders as he back handed J-Bone's mother and sent her flying off the bed. He looked over towards the nightstand and caught a glimpse of what she was up to.

"Oh you was gonna use that on me?" D.B. said, pointing at the exposed weapon in the drawer. She had gotten as close to opening the safe and lifting the top but that was about it.

She scurried to the corner, crying, holding her face.

"I'll take that, if you don't mind." D.B. said, as he removed the .38 revolver from the small safe and placed it in his right pants pocket. He already had a gun of his own. He aimed his weapon towards Momma Hicks and said, "Get up you old bitch and do as I say or you won't live to see the light of another day." Still scared and not knowing what's going on, she complied.

D.B. had her lay back down on the bed face down, arms behind her back and legs crossed as he duct tapped them both. Momma Hicks was scared for her life. She truly thought she was gonna die. She still had no clue what this was all about but had her suspicions. She felt it had something to do with the people who shot up her house not too long back. Maybe the exact same person coming back to finish the job. That day she remembered coming home to bullet holes in the wall and shattered glass. Jamal told her while she was out shopping someone had shot up the house. Lucky for her she wasn't there at the time.

D.B. put a final strip of duct tape over Momma Hicks' mouth to assure she couldn't be heard in the event she tried to scream or alert anyone that she was in danger. He then flung Momma Hicks' 115 lb body over his shoulders and left the house as quick as he entered.

"Blood, pop the trunk," D.B. said to the driver in the hot model as he approached walking fast towards the vehicle with Momma Hicks still draped over his shoulder. The young gangster popped the trunk as he placed J–Bone's mother inside and slammed it shut.

"80 seconds. Now that's how you pull off an abduction. Punch this mutha fucka Ru." D.B. said as he entered the car and they drove off. Shit was about to seriously get real. All bets were now off. D.B. just upped the ante by kidnapping J–Bone's mother which was about to take this war to a whole new level. Once J–Bone got word that his mother had been abducted, he would surely not rest until all parties involved paid with their lives.

XXX

"Hey baby, when you coming through ta check on a bitch? I haven't seen you in days." Jessica asked Dee over the phone as they spoke.

"Yeah I know, been a lot going on, business is hectic right now. But you're right, I have been missing in action lately. I'll come through tonight at 10:00 after I finish up with some business I currently have going on."

"Okay baby, sounds good to me." Jessica responded as they hung up the phone. Dee had his nose so far up Jessica's butt that he couldn't even sense the double cross. As sharp and on point as he was, he still wasn't sharp enough to see through Jessica's treachery.

Jessica hung up the phone and immediately called J-Bone. "Hello...10:00 tonight."

"Alright, good shit! I'll be there waiting." **CLICK**. As J-Bone hung up the phone all he could think about was how he was gonna take it to Dee.

XXX

"Blood, them niggas just got at me. I barely escaped with my life!" Killa said into the phone, speaking to J-Bone explaining what had happened and went down between him and 2-Face.

"Whaaaat, you bool Ru?" J-Bone responded.

"Yeah I'm good, just some gangta shit. Payback's a bitch and I'm ready ta fuck her! Straight like that. Them niggas got me fucked up East."

"No worries blood. I got some shit in motion as we speak. I was just finna call you Ru. That nigga Dee is about to be served to us on a silver platter."

"Word?" Killa responded, with a look of confusion and concern on his face.

"Yea dat! I got Jessica to set that nigga up. He pose ta show up at her place tonight at 10:00. He gonna get a rude awakening when he opens that door and see nothing but gun barrels staring back at him with nowhere to run."

"That's what the fuck I'm talking about, but you sure you can trust Jessica?"

"About as much as I can trust a hoodrat to

hold me down, stay faithful and ride with me through a bid, but it's a chance I'm willing to take. Been having my gunners out all week looking for this nigga. He doing a great job of hiding but now we're gonna seek out and destroy him. If Jessica betrays me, then she shall die, too."

J-Bone was cold blooded and calculated. He still loved Jessica, a lot, but not enough to let her live if she betrayed him...again.

"Okay well fuck it! If that's all we have to work with then that's all we have. Let's make this bitch do what it do and take it to this fuck boy," Killa responded.

"That's exactly what we're gonna do." J-Bone said, with a devilish smirk on his face.

"Alright, I'll see you tonight. B-up!"

"B-up Ru, tonight we put an end to this shit," J-Bone said as he hung up the phone.

XXX

This bitch think I'm stupid but I got something for her scandalous ass, Dee thought to himself. Jessica didn't know that since J-Bone's release from prison, Dee had been keeping a close tab on her. He had one of the young homies watch and tail her. At first it was because of the war and he didn't want her to get hurt or caught in the crossfire, but once the young homie called back with news that J-Bone had been seen going into her apartment and didn't leave for a few hours had Dee vexed.

He knew that Jessica's love for J-Bone ran deep. He was hoping he could change all that throughout the years J-Bone was locked up, through spoiling her with a lavish lifestyle, but money doesn't buy love so Jessica just used it as a great situation to take advantage.

Deep down, Dee always knew this and felt like he may be able to turn her around in time so fuck it. But the heart wants what the heart wants and Dee was not it. J-Bone was and this infuriated him.

Dee knew he was possibly walking into a trap but was well prepared. The war between J-Bone and Dee will come to a head tonight. Only one man will walk away with his life. Dee called and gave his crew a heads up. On the other side of town J-Bone did the same. Shit was about to go down in a real way. When it's all said and done, only one person would be left standing.

9 BETRAYAL

"Alright Blood check this out. We about to bring it to this nigga Dee in a real way. We got the upper hand which is the element of surprise but don't sleep, that nigga ain't stupid. Be on your A game and stay sharp like Velveeta," J-Bone instructed while standing in the kitchen of Jessica's apartment surrounding the dinner table with Killa and five other Skyline heavy hitters. The homies all nodded in agreement and strapped up.

"Now we wait," J-Bone said as he glanced at his watch to reveal the time which said 9:45. Dee was due over in 15 minutes.

Jessica sat in the back room on the bed looking nervous as all out doors. J-Bone's first instincts was to have her stay at her friend's house. Which friend? Didn't care, pick one, just as long as she was safe. But then he thought about what if Dee was smart enough to knock first to see if Jessica would open the door. Her not answering or coming to the door would be an instant red flag and could blow the mission.

"Alright blood take your positions, the nigga should be here any minute." J-Bone said as his soldiers took their positions, straps in hand and got ready. No sooner then they got into hiding...a knock at the door.

XXX

KNOCK KNOCK KNOCK, as the person in the hallway patiently waited for Jessica to answer and open the door, at which time, J-Bone silently instructed Jessica to open the door by waving his gun towards her and the door. Jessica nervously obliged, got up and went to do just that.

"Coming, be right there!" Jessica said as a

voice which sounded like Dee's on the other side of the door responded back,

"Okay baby." The sound of Dee's voice made the hair on the back of J-Bone raise up like a Pitbull in a dogfight. He pointed his weapon towards the door as he prepared and got ready for Jessica to open it. His soldiers did the same. Killa was stationed in the corner behind a recliner with his gun cocked. He prayed Dee brung 2-Face to the party so he could get some good old payback in the form of a bullet in his skull.

Jessica went to look through her peep hole before opening the door but could see nothing but blackness, like if someone had their finger over it. She instantly panicked.

"Baby, is that you?" Jessica asked, nervous with her hand on the door knob and the other on the lock.

"Yes it's me, who else is it gonna be? Now quit playing and open the door." The sound of Dee's voice put Jessica at ease. When she opened the door, a double barrel shotgun was staring her directly in the face. She didn't have a chance.

"**NOOOOO!!!!!!**" J-Bone hollered as Jessica's lifeless body hit the ground. She never saw it coming. A single shot to the chest from the double barrel was all it took ta send her flying and soul to her maker. Return fire erupted as the assailant was met with a barrage of bullets. Head, face and tousle rearranged from its original form. The gunman didn't even have a chance to return fire. As his dead body hit the floor, you could hear Dee say, "That's what you get for crossing me bitch! J-Bone, you next nigga."

J-Bone walked over to the body, gun in hand. The man on the ground was surely dead but yet he could still hear Dee talking. Now it was in the form of laughter. Furthermore, the body on the ground wasn't Dee. J-Bone kneeled down towards the body and sound of Dee's laughter. He reached into the gunman's coat pocket and pulled out a little mini digital recorder. When J-Bone rewinded and played it back, it was Dee's greeting at the front door.

"**Shit!** I told ya'll this nigga wasn't stupid. Now I done got Jessica killed." No sooner then J-Bone made that comment, a crash came through the window, followed by a flash boom which caught everyone by surprise and temporarily blinded everyone in the room except J-Bone because he was lucky enough to have been in the hallway standing over the body when the flash bomb came through the window. If he hadn't been out in that hallway, who knows what would've been his fate.

Young Skyline gang members from Dee's squad stormed the house. J-Bone quickly took cover. But not before letting off a hail of gun fire down the stairs. Two got hit instantly in the chest and hit the floor dead in their tracks. The others returned fire. J-Bone dived back in the house, hit the floor and crawled for cover like he was in a movie. But this was no movie. This was real life.

Killa and the homies on J-Bone's side started to slowly regain their site and got ready for war. Unfortunately, without the element of surprise on their side, they were more like sitting ducks in a small apartment waiting to be ambushed. Gunfire erupted on both sides as niggas entered the apartment. Killa noticed one of the gunmen pointing his

FRESH OUT

gun towards J-Bone who was scurrying around on the floor looking for cover. Killa quickly got off two shots from his Desert Eagle which sent him flying into the living room wall and crashing on the coffee table.

By this time J-Bone had found his way to the dining room where he quickly flipped over the dining table and made a shield to protect himself from the gunfire. **BOOM BOOM BOOM!!!** Three bullets came flying through the dining table and passed J-Bone's head. J-Bone returned fire but knew he had to find a better place to hide. This table wasn't gonna hold up. Another gunner entered the apartment but this one a little more on point than his Conrads, gun in hand, started strategically picking off J-Bone's men like he was a sniper in the army. Both sides was taking hits. Nothing went as planned. It was a free for all. At the rate this battle was going, there would be no winners, only losers. What started out as a bunch of good friends ended with a Set divided. Two sides cut from the same cloth now acting like sworn enemies. All behind the power of two men.

J-Bone took cover in the kitchen with one of the homies as he let off 50 shots within seconds from his fully automatic handgun. The gun and clip was modified to be fully automatic with an extended 100 round clip. He had two of them. He fired one until the clip was empty and reloaded in seconds with the spare clips in his tactical vest. Thank God he wore it because no sooner than he loaded his weapon, two shots from a shooter on Dee's side sent J-Bone flying into the nearest wall with him clutching his chest. It felt like he was hit with a baseball bat by Tony Gwen.

Might be hurt, but at least he was alive. Besides, adrenaline kept him from feeling or noticing much. He would definitely feel every bit of the aftermath later, though. J-Bone returned fire to the room. He didn't know who shot him. Didn't matter no way. Either you was with him or against him. He fired a few more shots towards the gun flashes across the room. Where some were panicking and just firing at everything moving, J-Bone was being calculated. Three more soldiers from Dee's side where hit. Two in the face and one in the chest. One of the bullets took one of the guys head clean off his shoulders as it exploded on impact. Shit was like World War 4 in this little ass apartment. **BOOM BOOM!!!**

"**Ahhh!!!**" This time the bullet met its mark as J-Bone yelled out "**I'm hit!**" J-Bone caught a bullet to his left shoulder. Lucky for him it was just a flesh wound. As he ducked for cover amongst the dead bodies on the floor, one in particular sent a cold chill down his body. As he looked directly to his left and saw Jessica's lifeless body staring back at him, eyes still open, he closed her eyes and said, "I'm sorry Babygirl. I never meant for you to go out like this."

J-Bone was torn. In one sense he always felt like Jessica deserved to pay for her treachery and in some ways with her life. The other side of him had way too much love for her to bring any harm her way in the form of death. Pay? Yes. With her life? No! Looking at Jessica lay there with no life in her body amped up the anger J-Bone was already feeling towards Dee.

"Blood, that's on Piru I'm ah kill this nigga if it's the last thing I do."

"Blood you alright?" Killa screamed out upon seeing J-Bone take a bullet to the shoulder.

"Yeah I'm bool. Just a flesh wound. It's gonna take a lot more than that to stop the Bone. Real shit! Head shots or nothing!" J-Bone responded.

"Then head shots...it shall be," a voice said as Dee entered the apartment with an AK.47 and lit up the room like a 4th of July celebration in the hood. Now shit just got real. They didn't call the AK a "chopper" for nothing. Everything that came in its path got chopped the fuck down. Everyone else's pistols and rifles didn't stand a chance.

J-Bone instantly knew he was outgunned and outmatched. But he was trapped in a small apartment on the second floor. He now regretted his decision to set up and meet Dee here. Dee was one step ahead of him and had flipped the script, using the set up to his own advantage. J-Bone seriously underestimated Dee's intelligence. He forgot they were cut from the same cloth. Shit, they used to be best friends. The number one thing in history that has split up the best of friendships and torn down empires...a WOMAN!

Jessica was the wedge that was formed between their friendship. Now these two who used to be conrads, were at each other's heads like the U.S. and Middle East.

"Blood! you wanna go to war with me?" Dee said, as he continued firing the automatic weapon laying any and everything down moving in the apartment. J-Bone and Killa ran for the back room just missing being hit by gunfire as bullet whizzed by their heads. Everyone else in the apartment was dead. This included the soldiers on Dee's side as well. The only 3 remaining was Dee, J-Bone and Killa.

"Come on out and play you fuckin pussy. I thought you wanted to rock with the big dogs?" **TAT,TAT,TAT,TAT,TAT,TAT!!!!** Dee said as he continued firing into the bedroom Killa and J-Bone ran into. J-Bone closed the door but knew it was pretty much pointless as the AK.47 bullets ripped through the door turning it into swiss cheese.

"Blood, you alright?" asked Killa.

"Yeah I'm bool but we gotta get outta here."

"Who you telling?" Killa responded. Just then, J-Bone walked to the window, opened it up and peeped outside. It was a long way down. He was all out of options as he could hear Dee approaching, still firing off shots like a Muslim in Bagdad.

"Blood, we gon have ta jump," J-Bone said to Killa. Killa was afraid of heights so he wasn't feeling that shit. But soon as the last round of shots blew the bedroom door off the hinges, Killa was the first one smoking out the window. He landed hard and sprung his ankle on contact. He was so pumped with adrenaline that at the time he didn't even notice. J-Bone followed next as he climbed out the window and hung from the ledge before letting go and dropping to the ground. He landed with a little more spring in his step which kept him from breaking or spraining anything as well on impact.

No sooner than he landed, Dee was at the window letting off shots. Killa fired back which gave J-Bone just enough cover fire to get up and seek refuge. Dee reloaded his AK.47 and went to fire out the window but no one was there. J-Bone and Killa had got ghost.

"Mark ass niggas." Dee said out loud to himself as he scanned the area and continued to see nothing. Just then sirens could be heard in the background. A clear indication that it was time to kick rocks. Dee left the apartment the same way he came and disappeared into the night. Yeah Dee may have won the battle, but the war was far from over.

10 REDRUM

J-Bone and Killa ran a few blocks down Skyline Drive and stopped at the park to catch their breath. Police sirens could be heard headed towards Jessica's apartment. J-Bone knew he had to get off the streets and fast. "Come on blood, we gotta continue moving," J-Bone said, as him and Killa cut through Skyline Park and headed through the back streets to one of the homie's house who lived on Wedgewood named Rock.

Rock was a music producer who lived in the Set. He grew up in the heart of Skyline all his life. Right up the street and around the corner from the park. All the homies hung out at the park. Especially in the 80's and 90's. The Set was hella active and the park was where it was at. Rock was never really officially put onto the set. He was more of what you'd call an affiliate. He was guilty by association but that was about it. He wasn't about to pick up nobody's gun, go slang nobody's dope, put in no type of work, see not one bar in prison but knew everybody. Some of the young homies from the Set that rapped used to go over his house and make mixtapes. Some would go on to be hood classics.

J-Bone and Killa arrived at Rock's house just as the ghetto bird (police helicopter) was hovering over the Set. Once the bird had an eye on you there was no place to hide. All one could do at that point was give up. Since giving up was not an option, J-Bone and Killa made their way to the homie's house quick.

KNOCK KNOCK KNOCK!!! "**Blood open up!**" J-Bone said as he frantically knocked on Rock's door.

"Who is it knockin on my door like the fuckin police?" Rock answered from the other side of the door walking towards it to see who it was.

"Blood open the door, it's me, J-Bone and Killa. Hurry up Ru, it's an emergency. I been shot and Popo's out here looking for us." Rock opened the door in shock to see a wounded J-Bone and frantic Killa injured and sweating profusely.

"Damn what happened, ya'll okay?" asked Rock.

"Blood, do we look okay?" asked Killa. Of course that was a rhetorical question. "Quit asking dumb ass questions and let us in." J-Bone and Killa pushed past Rock before he even had a chance to respond or let them in. Lucky for them, Rock's mom was out for the evening.

"Damn, what happened?" asked Rock.

"Nothing a nigga can't handle," said J-Bone. "Get me some water, a large bowl and peroxide. Also, see if your mom has some bandages." Rock's mom was a registered nurse so J-Bone knew she had to at the very least kept a First Aid Kit. He was right in his thinking because Rock disappeared to the back only to emerge with a full fledged big boy First Aid Kit, with any and everything you could imagine in it. Rock examined J-Bone's flesh wound.

"Looks like the bullet went straight through," Rock said while reaching into the First Aid Kit to retrieve a few swabs and peroxide. He cleaned the cut then wrapped it up. Killa pulled back the curtain and peeped out the window. **POW!** Clear through the eyeball a .38 slug ripped through the skull of Killa as he flew back five feet and landed next to J-Bone and Rock. He was dead before his body touched the ground.

"**NOOOOOO!!!!!!!**" That yell from J-Bone was met by a barrage of bullets from outside. Enough was enough. Too many had died. The Set was divided and no one could be trusted. Best friends who grew up together became overnight enemies. All of this flashed in J-Bone's head as he picked up his gun with tunnel vision. Jessica...Killa...the dead homies left in the apartment. He knew he couldn't let them all die in vain. Rock panicked when he saw Killa's dead body hit the floor and ran for the back. He wasn't bout dat life and wasn't about to start pretending like he was. J-Bone however, didn't give a fuck. He was done running. This time bullets will be met head on. This was Rocky One with a gun. As J-Bone stood up in rage, gun in hand, the front door flew open and there stood Dee. Both men looked at each other for a split second. With a devilish grin on both, they simultaneously started busting at each other. **BOOM BOOM BOOM! TAT TAT TAT TAT TAT!!!!!**

Shit was like a movie, a whole lot of gunfire but neither one of them got hit. Crazy part is they was shooting at each other in full view with no cover like that scene with Neo and the dude chasing him on The Matrix. Now they were damn near face to face with both guns drawn at each other's head. **Click Click!**

Both guns empty. That meant good old hand to hand combat. J-Bone reacted the quickest with a swift right to Dee's jaw, snapping his neck back on impact. Dee took the hit like a champ in a world class fight and responded with two punches of his own. The first one missed but the second hit his mark.

They both squared off and regained composure. **WAP WAP!!!**

"That's all you got blood? Nigga you hit like a bitch!" Dee responded to the two shots he just ate like breakfast toast.

"Nah, that was just the warm-up." J-Bone rushed Dee like a UFC fighter and swooped him up by the legs. It only took a split second to send him up over and straight on his back. The impact knocked the wind out of him as he clutched his mid-section. J-Bone took full advantage of the situation and started kicking him in the ribs. The last kick broke one. Dee knew he had to get his ass up or he was a dead man. Better to die standing, but he had no intentions on dying. Dee was a dirty nigga, not to mention there was no such thing as a fair fight. Slowly, Dee reached for a concealed knife he had strategically placed near his ankle. J-Bone never saw it coming. As he reached to grab Dee, his left hand was met with the blade of a butterfly knife.

"**AHHH!!!!!!!!**" J-Bone yelled. The knife went straight through his hand. You could literally see the blade sticking out the back. This gave

Dee time to get up and regroup. Not much though as J-Bone backhanded Dee, knife still in hand as he stuck him on impact. The point of the blade went straight through Dee's right cheek.

Dee screamed out in pain holding his face as crimson blood began to trickle down his face. J-Bone pulled the knife out of his hand with one quick jerk. "**AHHHH...SHIT!**" The pain was excruciating, but at least he had it out.

"Yeah nigga, ain't no fun when the rabbit got the gun," J-Bone said, wielding the shiny knife with a slight smirk on his face, a devilish grin if you will. Dee quickly took off his shirt and wrapped it around his arm like he'd seen in the movies. Unfortunately for him, this was no movie. J-Bone lunged at Dee with the knife as he tried to use the wrapped arm as a shield. Needless to say, the knife went straight through the shirt and cut Dee's wrist, slicing one of his veins in the process. The shirt instantly started to soak up with Dee's blood. If he didn't do something fast he would bleed to death. Not to mention, J-Bone still had the knife. Before Dee could think about his next move, J-Bone went in for the kill. Knife in hand, he rushed Dee like a linebacker. J-Bone's time in prison made him quite handy with a knife. He had to give quite a few inmates the business while doing his time up state.

J-Bone reversed the knife so the blade was positioned towards the floor and started throwing hammer fist. He stuck Dee a few more times in various parts of his body as he tried to gut this nigga like a fish.

"Ugghh!!!" Dee screamed out in agony as J-Bone stuck him in the chest, three inches away from his heart. Dee started coughing up blood, a clear sign of internal bleeding. J-Bone stood up over Dee's body to watch him slowly die. Dee started laughing while still coughing up blood.

"What the fuck you laughing at dead man? Looks ta me like you lost this war."

"Oh...did I?" Dee responded back, leaving J-Bone confused.

"A blind man can see how this is gonna play out."

"Yea, well, I guess that's why they're

called...BLIND!" Dee said and started laughing hysterically like the Joker on Batman. J-Bone still didn't catch the joke. What the fuck was so funny? Just then, J-Bone's cellphone rang. He actually forgot he had it on him. He was about to pay it no mind and let it go to voicemail when Dee said, "you might wanna get that playa," before taking his last breath and fading off into darkness.

"Thank goodness, I was tired of hearing that mother fucka's mouth," J-Bone said to himself before hitting the answer button on his phone. "Hello...who this?"

"D.B. nigga! I got someone here that wants to talk to you."

"Baby help, please help!!!"

"MOMMA???"

"YES BABY, IT'S ME...I BEEN KIDNAPPED!"

IF YOU ENJOYED READING
"FRESH OUT"
PLEASE LEAVE A REVIEW ON AMAZON.COM
http://ow.ly/JggvZ

ABOUT THE AUTHOR

Upon being released from prison in 2011, Caujuan turned his life around, created Uprock Publications and penned his first book, "Let Me Pimp Or Let Me Die," which was an instant success and 5 star hit on Amazon. He then followed up with his second and third book "Let Me Pimp Or Let Me Die 2" and "Cooking With Weed." Caujuan has also signed other successful authors to his company as well. You can find Caujuan on Facebook under "Caujuan" as well as on all other popular social networks under the same name. If you'd like to learn more about Caujuan Akim Mayo, then feel free to visit www.uprockpublications.com.

ALSO AVAILABLE

When his father passed at 12, Mr. Terrell Washington grew up fast and survived the dangerous streets of East Chicago, Indiana. After finding out his deceased father left him a large inheritance, he decided to leave for California and achieve his dream of becoming a published Author. However, the land of Hollywood stars was soon transformed into a maze of unforeseen obstacles he never expected on his way to the top. How will it play out??? Will he achieve his dream, or will it be shattered into a nightmare of failure.

A hard life in the inner city. Made it through. About to prepare for the next step of most young men. College. That was all until one fateful night to where freedom was taken away. Now, in the battle of his young life, a young man has two options. Die in prison, or snitch and possibly get another chance. Either choice will draw consequences, but what will he choose??? What wounds will be healed, and what wounds will be re-opened???

Xavier Sands and Danielle Seville meet at the grand opening of Xavier's nightclub, and it happens to be his birthday. Not to be left out, Danielle is celebrating her birthday as well. As the two grow closer, wedges are driven between them behind the scenes, by their own mothers!

Xavier and Danielle both work for King Kole Konners, in different venues, but when the King is shot, all bets are off. The kingdom having just survived the Chase St. John mutiny in South Nubia, is rocked once again. The assassin begins picking off the King's top people, leading to Danielle being kidnapped.

UPROCK PUBLICATIONS PRESENTS

LET ME PIMP
OR
LET ME DIE
=Till Game Do Us Part=

a novel by
CAUJUAN AKIM MAYO

Ricky Walters grew up in the gritty streets of San Diego, California. Upon quitting his security job, he meets an ex pimp named Trust who teaches him everything about the pimp game. Ricky ends up turning out a young Asian girl named Yuki, changes his name to Jackpot, and jumps knee deep in the pimp game. Jackpot makes a conscious decision to become the biggest pimp to ever play the game and goes cross country. Here is where Jackpot finds himself getting money, ducking the police, feuding with haters, vindictive females, snitches, and eventually doing time in the penitentiary.

Let Me Pimp Or Let Me Die 2, tells the story of a few female workers in the "Game," told through their lives as you see, and find out what motivates a woman to start hoe'n and sell her body. Re-visit some of your favorite characters from part 1 and see what drove them into the lifestyle that they chose. Each story different, but ultimately the same.

Graphic and not for the faint of heart, the scenes take place in a realistic setting with many twists n turns you won't see coming. Find out how F.A.B killed Sunshine and what happened in those last moments. How Green Eyes got hooked on drugs and the real reason she left Jackpot for dead in prison. Or the number one question...Will Jackpot Return To The Game?

Wake n Bake the natural way. Weed consumption through digestion is a lot healthier than smoking it, which is why we put together this book of tasty meals with a 420 kick to keep you happy, smiling and feeling good! From breakfast, lunch, dinner to dessert we got you covered. Enjoy some weed laced french toast for breakfast. Craving a light snack? Try some of our weed hummus. End the night with a homemade weed pizza and cheesecake for dessert. We even have a recipe for cooking oil and weed butter. Over 30 different recipes to choose from. Meals so quick and easy to make, you'll wonder why you didn't pick up this book sooner. Simple everyday recipes made easy will have you feeling like a pro in the kitchen! No more having to buy overpriced edibles from the dispensary. Now you can make all those delicious treats yourself.

UPROCK AUDIOBOOKS

Don't have the time to read? Well, we have the solution. Pick up your audio version of "Let Me Pimp Or Let Me Die," the book by Caujuan Akim Mayo that started it all. Listen to this action packed audio book, loaded with special sound effects and cinematic music for dramatic effect, like no other audio book you've ever heard before. This is the audio book, that changed the game and set the bar.

<u>COMING SOON</u>
BANDAGES 2 - FALL 2015

- Website: www.uprockpublications.com
- Emails: uprockp@gmail.com
- Facebook: uprockpublications
- Twitter: uprockpub
- Contact: (619) 259-0298